'Does he

The questio so
bizarre Tess

'Does who k

'The man yo

Tess was so dumbfounded she could only stare at him. Eduardo was on his feet, taking the baby and holding her gently against his shoulder, rubbing her back as if he'd comforted a thousand babies in his time.

Tess looked at them, and tears pricked her eyes again, but she was damned if she was going to cry. She was strong, and independent, and she was going to be the best mother in the world to Charlotte. So she couldn't go getting tearful over the sight of the man she loved holding her baby.

'No, the man I love doesn't know I love him. He doesn't have an inkling.'

He stared at her, the light tan on her face making her eyes seem greener tonight, the long hair all tousled from sleep, the full mouth that had fed on his with such passion— Dio! Could it be? But why would she not say? Because he'd told her not to expect anything from him... And what *had* he to offer her?

This answer came more slowly.

Love! He could offer her love.

Meredith Webber says of herself, 'Some years ago, I read an article which suggested that Mills & Boon were looking for new medical authors. I had one of those "I can do that" moments, and gave it a try. What began as a challenge has become an obsession, though I do temper the "butt on seat" career of writing with dirty but healthy outdoor pursuits, fossicking through the Australian Outback in search of gold or opals. Having had some success in all of these endeavours, I now consider I've found the perfect lifestyle.'

Recent titles by the same author:

THE NURSE HE'S BEEN WAITING FOR*
HIS RUNAWAY NURSE
THE SPANISH DOCTOR'S CONVENIENT BRIDE
A FATHER BY CHRISTMAS
BRIDE AT BAY HOSPITAL
THE DOCTOR'S MARRIAGE WISH*

Crocodile Creek: 24-Hour Rescue

A
PREGNANT NURSE'S
CHRISTMAS WISH

BY
MEREDITH WEBBER

MILLS & BOON®
Pure reading pleasure

First published in Great Britain 2007
Harlequin Mills & Boon Limited,
Eton House, 18-24 Paradise Road, Richmond, Surrey TW9 1SR

© Meredith Webber 2007

ISBN: 978 0 263 85283 7

Set in Times Roman 10½ on 12¾ pt
03-1207-49341

Printed and bound in Spain
by Litografia Rosés, S.A., Barcelona

A
PREGNANT NURSE'S
CHRISTMAS WISH

CHAPTER ONE

THE WOMAN SPLASHED through the shallows on the far side of the lagoon, her feet lifting high as she ran so the sprays of clear water sparkled like dewdrops around long, pale legs, while the wind whipped the fine white shirt she wore over her bikini across her body, moulding itself against her—

Protruding belly?

Eduardo picked up the binoculars that lay on the table beside his sun lounge and put them to his eyes, focussing in on the figure in white.

Protruding belly all right. The woman was pregnant. Noticeably pregnant.

Uneasily aware that he might be spying on her, he replaced the binoculars on the table and frowned at the now smaller figure on the far side of the blue lagoon.

He'd assumed, when he'd first seen her, she must be Mathilde's friend, the nurse she'd trained with in Brisbane, here to take over the running of the clinic while Mathilde took her mother to the mainland for chemotherapy. But Mathilde was unlikely to have asked a pregnant woman to take her place, even for a short time.

Unless she hadn't known…

It would have been easy enough for the woman to deceive her, knowing Mathilde was leaving before her arrival.

Deceit and women! Would the two words be linked for ever in his mind?

He sighed, intelligent enough to know he couldn't generalise—too intelligent to think all women were deceitful. Caroline, who'd started the controversy at the research lab that had led to the court case, and Ilse, his ex-wife, were more the exception than the norm, surely. It was just the fact he was so closely linked to both that he found it hard not to look for it in other women, not to feel distrust.

The woman currently under suspicion had cast aside her shirt and was now swimming across the lagoon with long, strong strokes, her wet hair trailing darkly behind her, casting a shadow on the pale skin of her back.

She'd burn for sure.

And had no one told her this small island on the far side of the lagoon was private land?

Out of the water now, she was lying on her back, moving her legs and arms lazily through the white coral sand like a child making a snow angel.

Very pregnant!

Irresponsible, if she *was* Mathilde's friend, coming to an isolated group of islands in her condition.

Irresponsible, lying in the tropical sun when her pale skin would burn in minutes.

Yet something in the way she'd splashed through the water—something in the sheer joy of her movements—had awoken a response within him so, although he strode across his veranda and down the steps, following the gritty path to the beach, the reproof he'd thought to utter weakened on his tongue.

He'd introduce himself instead. Check she was Mathilde's friend. Welcome her to Tihoroa, act polite then find someone else to take Mathilde's place.

Someone responsible.

Someone not pregnant.

But first he'd be polite.

Or he would have if she'd been there. He stared at the angel impression she'd left in the sand, then looked across the lagoon, to see her disappearing into the shadows of the fringing palm trees, pulling on her shirt as she went.

It *was* paradise, Tess mentally confirmed as she made her way along the path beneath the palm trees to the thatch-roofed hut that would be her home for the next four weeks. Warm sun, white sand, deep blue-green water, the wide smiles of greeting she'd received at the tiny airport—it was a gift from heaven, time out from the turmoil that had begun not when she'd decided to use Grant's last gift to her and have his child, but when she'd told both of their families.

'Excuse me.'

The voice, deep and dark and huskily accented, made her turn.

Sun, sand, water and a pirate? Not much taller than she was, but with knotted muscles pushing at his water-slicked skin, deeply tanned, with wet, bedraggled, over-long, dark hair, and eyes so intense a brown they appeared black, set beneath frowning brows.

He even had the requisite pirate scar, running from the corner of his left eye to the lobe of his ear, and a golden ring gleaming in one ear.

Tess stared at him, aware of her rudeness but unable to

stop herself, feeling a thud of apprehension in her chest even though she knew he couldn't possibly be a pirate.

Pirates didn't exist…

'You are Mathilde's friend?'

'Tess Beresford,' Tess said, offering her hand, ignoring every instinct in her body warning her to beware of pirates.

'I am Eduardo del Riga,' the pirate said, taking her hand and confirming her instincts as a tingle not unlike an electric shock jolted along her nerves.

'Not a pirate but a doctor.' Tess managed to inject a lightness she was far from feeling into her voice as she retrieved her hand and put it behind her back so she couldn't touch the moisture beading on his shoulder.

'Not a pirate?' the deep voice echoed, no hint of a smile on his well-shaped lips or lurking in the dark eyes.

'Just a silly thought I had when I turned and saw you,' Tess explained, trying to sound like a sensible nursing sister and not some romantic dreamer who met pirates under palm trees. 'The sun, the sand, the island atmosphere—pirates just came to mind.'

'Of course,' Eduardo said politely, but Tess could almost see his true reaction—*What an idiot*—in a bubble above his head.

'Did Mathilde know you were pregnant?'

The question, bearing the overtones of other people's criticism, made thoughts of pirates flee. Tess straightened her shoulders and fought to keep her hands from curling protectively around her belly.

'Why do you ask?' she demanded, aware of uncharacteristic rudeness, but then, his question had been equally rude.

'Because your condition surprised me.'

He was frowning at her but before she could explain, he spoke again.

'I would have thought a woman, what, six months pregnant, would think twice before coming to such an isolated place. And I would have thought your husband would have advised against it also.'

Not my husband, but my parents, and Dan, and even Mathilde when I told her, Tess acknowledged privately to herself. But now, with one more person ranged against her, she stiffened her spine and tilted her chin, the better to deliver a full-force Beresford glare at this presumptuous man.

'It's seven months, not six—thirty-one weeks, to be exact,' she said coolly, 'And, yes, Mathilde knew, and she did have some concerns about me coming, but I reminded her that pregnancy is not an illness and it hasn't stopped me doing my job on the mainland so I can't see that it would affect me doing it on Tihoroa. Particularly as running the clinic isn't a particularly arduous task. According to Mathilde, the islanders are very healthy so most of what I'll have to do is supervise the other staff who could probably run it on their own. Then there's the fact that women on Tihoroa have babies all the time, as you, Dr del Riga, well know, so the isolation story doesn't work. And, finally, I don't have a husband.'

She'd ticked off each point on her fingers as she'd made it, and now used that hand to give a small salute before turning her back on her inquisitor and marching on towards her temporary home, aware she shouldn't have lost her temper—shouldn't have got off on the wrong foot with this man. But his criticism had echoed Dan's words when he'd seen her off at the airport that morning—stupid, irresponsible, stubborn, single—and while she'd brushed aside

Dan's arguments, refusing to rise to his bait, the injustice of it must have been festering inside her, awaiting release onto the head of the unsuspecting Eduardo.

He followed, although she couldn't hear his footsteps in the soft sand, just felt his presence in a rippling of nerves along her backbone and an awareness skittering beneath her skin.

The path led past her house to the main village and the clinic so he was probably on his way there, but when she turned towards her hut he reached out and touched her arm.

'It was insensitive, my question?' he asked, the husky voice sending new tremors down her spine. 'I didn't intend it to be, but your condition startled me. I worried for you.'

Near-black eyes scanned her face, and met hers with an intensity she could almost feel. It wasn't an apology but it came close, and deep down she knew she should be the one apologising.

'You worry for everyone, from what Mathilde has told me,' Tess said, trying to lighten the atmosphere between them—trying, also, to dismiss the uncertainty she was feeling in front of him. Coming to Tihoroa was all about getting over uncertainty. It was about reaffirming her decision to have Grant's child and regathering her inner strength, confidence and hard-won independence—all attributes she would need if she was to be the best possible mother to her child.

Eduardo shook his head, dismissing her remark, wondering what it was about this woman that had got so quickly under his skin. It had to be the pregnancy. His own dreams of having children—his dreams of family—had been shattered when he'd discovered Ilse's infidelity. Now here was this woman, carrying a precious child and behaving as if…

As if it was normal?

Of course it was normal!

Maybe the explanation for his concern was the one the visitor had offered. He *did* have an over-developed sense of responsibility, but usually only over the islanders. Care for their well-being had been bred into him, as strong as the genes that had given him dark hair and eyes.

'The islanders don't need me worrying over them these days,' he said, meeting the woman's clear grey-green eyes. 'They've always been a proud and independent people, but now they're proving to have great business sense as well. Tihoroan pearls are sought after by the world's best jewellers.'

Her pale pink lips slid into a smile, parting slightly to reveal strong white teeth with just the hint of a gap between the front two.

'And by wealthy women everywhere,' she added, then she lifted her right hand to show him a small baroque pearl set in a simple silver band. 'I was lucky to get one before they became so well known. Mathilde gave me this back when we were training together.'

It was only natural he take her hand to examine the pearl, the pinkish lustre confirming it as Tihoroan, but he'd no sooner felt the slim cool fingers resting on his palm than he regretted it. Her touch galvanised his blood, sending messages straight to his groin. He, who hadn't lusted after a woman in years, was suddenly on fire.

'It's a good pearl,' he managed to say, dropping the hand but finding no relief from the heat within him.

Tess was glad he'd dropped her hand. It was disturbing enough standing close to him, but that sensation of uneasiness had been multiplied a thousandfold when he'd touched her.

'I must shower and change,' she told him, turning again towards her hut. 'According to the schedule Mathilde left for me, I'm to meet the staff at lunch in the clinic dining room at one.'

'I will escort you there.'

It was a statement that brooked no argument, so there'd be no escaping the disturbing man.

'You will be ready in half an hour?' he added.

'Thank you,' she said weakly—after all, he *was* her boss.

He was sitting on the step when she emerged exactly thirty minutes later. She'd dressed in dark blue calf-length trousers and a loose blue and white checked shirt that floated down over her bulge. Not a uniform, but plain enough clothes to pass for one, although, when she saw Eduardo del Riga again, she realised wearing more clothes did nothing to stop the quiver of excitement he caused.

Pregnancy hormones, she assured herself as he rose to his feet and, with a small bow that with another man might have seemed staged but with him was politely courteous, waved her towards the path.

He too had more clothes on, a faded blue chambray shirt over the long shorts he'd been wearing earlier. The shorts had dried out now, but it was far from formal doctor wear, although, Tess realised as she walked along the sandy path beneath the palm trees, mainland attire would look ridiculous in this place.

'Eduardo!'

The panicked cry came from somewhere up ahead, and as the doctor strode off Tess saw a tall islander, his face, even at a distance, distorted with fear, while his arms cradled a woman close to his chest.

'It's Berthe. The pains have begun but she says they are not the right pains.'

Tess hurried to catch up as Eduardo ushered the pair into the low clinic building.

Two young nurses Tess had met earlier were bustling about, one holding open a door into an examination room, the other searching through the file folders stacked in shelves behind the clinic's reception counter. As Tess passed, the nurse found the file she sought, clipped the pages to a backing board and turned to follow Tess into the examination room.

'Multiparous, thirty-five weeks, isn't it, Berthe?' the doctor was saying as he helped the man lay the woman on an examination table, and then fitted a blood-pressure cuff to her arm. 'Check the foetal heart rate for me, please, Sister.'

Great! Tess's introductory tour of the clinic was supposed to take place *after* lunch. But she'd sensed disapproval of her condition in Eduardo del Riga so now was as good a time as any to prove she was up to the task of running the clinic for the four weeks Mathilde would be away.

The younger of the two nurses, Janne, wheeled a small machine close to the table. Fortunately it was the same type of electronic foetal monitor Tess had used at her last job, and she placed the transducer on the woman's abdomen and handed Berthe the lead, asking her to press the button on it when she felt foetal movement.

'It's not the baby moving around, it's the pain,' the woman gasped, but Tess was staring worriedly at the monitor. The FHR was far too low, and when Berthe did feel a movement and press the button, the foetal heart rate barely responded.

'Where's the pain?' Eduardo was asking, while Tess

scribbled a note to him on a blank chart sheet she'd found beside the monitor.

'It's everywhere,' Berthe told him, then she winced as he probed her swollen abdomen. 'Really sore all over my belly but contractions as well.'

She let out a shrill cry as a contraction ripped through her, apparently to prove her point.

Eduardo continued to examine her, touching her gently, checking dilatation of her cervix—none evident—setting an IV catheter into place on her hand, taking two vials of blood, which he handed to Janne with a crisp command, then starting fluid running through the port.

Excusing himself to Berthe, he drew Tess a little to one side and told her his findings.

'Any ideas?' he asked quietly. Not a test, but information-seeking, his concern for the woman apparent in his face.

'Abruptio placentae?' Tess offered, remembering a woman with similar symptoms from her recent term in the O and G department at the hospital. 'It seems like classic symptoms with the pain and contractions.'

'There's no bleeding,' Eduardo said, 'but, yes, the placenta could have detached high up—above the foetal sac—and bleeding into the epithelial tissues would cause the contractions. From what I remember, ultrasound is no help in confirming it.'

Tess nodded her agreement, then pictured the problem in her mind, seeing the placenta pulled away from the uterine wall, the blood making a dark shadow there.

'We could use an intra-uterine pressure catheter to measure the intra-uterine pressure, which is another indicator, but I'm worried about the FHR. It's very low and not responding to contractions. Will you fly her out?'

She knew the community had an arrangement with the Australian flying doctor service to airlift emergency cases from the islands.

Eduardo shook his head.

'Two hours' flying time for them to get here, and that's after they're airborne, then a two-hour flight back. With the FHR already non-reassuring, that's far too long to wait.'

'You'll do a Caesar here?'

Tess hoped she didn't sound as panicky as she felt. Eduardo, she knew from Mathilde, had been a physician before he'd turned to research and though he'd been back on the island for a year and treating any islander who needed basic medical care, this might be a job for an expert.

Theoretically every student who went through med school had to perform a certain number of Caesarean deliveries during their training, but how many did they perform once they'd qualified? Unless intent on pursuing the O and G specialty, very few.

'Don't look so worried,' he said, touching her lightly on the arm. 'I have a great DVD on the subject and a screen already set up in Theatre. We'll follow it step by step.'

He *had* to be joking!

But if he was, he'd must be a master poker player because no hint of humour showed on his face.

'Besides,' he continued calmly, 'from what I've read of your qualifications, you could probably do it yourself. When did you last assist in a Caesar?'

'Last week,' she told him. 'I've been in the O and G theatre for the last few months. I love theatre work and take a theatre rotation whenever I can.'

'Well, there you are,' Eduardo announced with enough confidence to cause Tess even more alarm. 'Between you and the DVD—Caesars for Dummies—we should manage perfectly well.'

Was he *mad*?

He'd left her side to speak to Berthe and her husband, Albert, and Tess watched. She heard the calm confidence in his voice as he explained what they suspected had happened, before telling them what he intended doing. She decided the talk of 'Caesars for Dummies' *had* to have been a joke.

Either that or he was an excellent doctor, who knew the importance of patient confidence before even the most minor procedure, and no matter what doubts he had himself about his ability, he made sure none of them were transmitted to the patient.

He sent the second nurse scurrying from the room, and when Janne returned with the blood-test results told her to prepare the theatre for a Caesar.

'You want me to do the anaesthetic?' the young woman asked, and Eduardo flashed a smile at her.

'That's why we sent you to America—not just to look at film stars,' he told her, teasing her yet touching her shoulder for further reassurance. 'But you won't be on your own. I'll be there to guide you, and Sister Beresford here is an experienced theatre nurse so she could probably do an easy anaesthetic like this one.'

Janne squared her shoulders and nodded her head at Eduardo.

'I can do it,' she said, then she crossed to where Berthe lay and spoke to her in low tones, picking up her chart and checking things off on it at the same time, taking her own set of observations, asking when Berthe had last eaten, then explaining to Berthe she'd be giving her an injection of premed to make her sleepy, although the actual an-aesthetic wouldn't be given until she was in Theatre so she was under for the shortest possible time.

Tess was impressed by the young woman's competence and intrigued by the training.

'A course in America?' she asked Eduardo as they scrubbed together in the small room attached to the pristine theatre at the back of the clinic.

'There are similar courses now in Australia for nurses who wish to become nurse practitioners, but islanders have a mind set that things in America must surely be better, so it is more impressive to them to have someone train over there.'

'Train as an anaesthetist?' Tess pursued, although she was fascinated by the insight into the islander psyche.

'In basic anaesthetics,' Eduardo explained. 'As you know, before the days when just about all patients are transferred out of country hospitals to larger centres, nurses in small hospitals often gave anaesthesia, under the guidance of the local doctor. I could have trained Berthe myself, but people will be more confident of her skills—'

'Because she learnt them in America,' Tess finished for him, shaking her head in amazement.

Then she registered the other part of his conversation.

'*You* could have trained her? I thought your specialist training had been as a physician, not as an anaesthetist or a surgeon.'

Eduardo was holding up his hands for gloves and helping the nurse fit them on as he nodded in reply.

'I didn't realise until I made the decision to return to Tihoroa just how narrow my medical focus had become,' he said.

He glanced sideways at her.

'You know I was in research?'

Six words but so loaded with implications Tess could feel their weight in the air.

She kept her answer to a simple 'Yes.'

He nodded again, and continued.

'So I hadn't done a lot of hands-on medicine for years. I knew I couldn't offer the Tihoorans half a doctor, so before returning I did six months in a major hospital, swapping between the emergency department and O and G, knowing these would be the skills I would most require.'

Subject closed, Tess guessed as he strode away, giving orders for fresh frozen plasma and cryoprecipitate to be brought to Theatre. But as she followed him into the theatre, she wondered about those six months he'd spent in a hospital, working the two specialties that required the most overtime and night duty.

As well as learning, had he been working hard so he hadn't had to think about the pending court case? Banned from his laboratory and the work he'd pursued for years— work he'd loved, according to Mathilde—had he sought escape from worry in the busy ER and O and G departments of a major city hospital?

Berthe was ready for them, a catheter draining her bladder, a drip running into her arm and leads snaking off her body. Two nurses stood behind prepared trolleys, one holding operating instruments, swabs and sutures, the other all the requirements for the newborn once he or she had been delivered.

Janne stood by Berthe's head, checking the leads from Berthe to the monitor, obviously anxious, although her hands moved without the slightest tremor.

And Eduardo *was* standing in front of a monitor, but the

information he was checking was far from Caesars for
Dummies. In fact, he was listening to the calm, confident
voice of a youngish-looking man, and Tess realised he had
a live link to a specialist.

'There could be a lot of blood escape at any time during
the operation,' the talking head was saying. 'If not when
you make the incision through the abdominal wall, then
when you deliver the placenta. You've blood on hand?'

'Fresh frozen plasma,' Eduardo told him, and Tess
shook her head in wonder at the marvels of modern technology, that they could be on a small island in the vast
Pacific Ocean yet be chatting to a specialist in a city hospital in Australia.

Or was the man's accent American?

He was assuring Eduardo that was a good choice because it had all the procoagulants.

'Although,' he reminded Eduardo, 'it has no platelets so
full blood might be necessary later.'

Definitely Australian, Tess decided, before switching
her mind back to the patient. It was time to begin.

Eduardo moved into position, checked Berthe's status
with Janne and took up a scalpel. Tess picked up a swab
and doused it in antiseptic then waited for Eduardo's order.

'A transverse incision low down, I think,' he said to
Tess. 'Although this is Berthe's fourth child, she might
want another later on and a low incision gives her more
chance of a vaginal delivery next time.'

Tess swabbed Berthe's stomach, low down where
Eduardo would make the incision, then stood by to clamp
or cauterise blood vessels for him as he cut through the skin
and muscles of the abdominal wall, exposing the peritoneum, the membrane enclosing the abdominal organs.

Another transverse incision, which Tess held apart with retractors.

Then, very gently, Eduardo moved the bladder to one side so the uterus was in full view. It was a dark blue, almost purple colour, indicative of bleeding into its muscular wall, evidence of abruptio placentae.

He made a small incision, slowly deepening it until Tess caught a glimpse of the membranes of the inner lining and the foetal sac beneath them.

Eduardo was talking all the time and Tess realised he was relaying his movements to the man on the monitor, who only occasionally made a remark.

'Going deeper,' Eduardo said. He moved the scalpel and blood gushed like a fountain, so Tess had to mop first Eduardo's face then the open wound, holding thick swabs to the incision to absorb as much blood as possible.

'I suppose there's some satisfaction in being right,' Eduardo muttered to the man on the screen as he left the theatre to clean up and reglove before proceeding.

Tess continued her mopping-up operations, glancing anxiously at the monitor from time to time. But in spite of the evidence of haemorrhage, Berthe's blood pressure remained relatively stable.

Eduardo returned, nodded his thanks to Tess, then continued, using his fingers to separate the outer uterine membranes and expand the incision before slipping one hand in to find the baby's head.

Tess handed him obstetric forceps, and within seconds the little head was safely delivered.

'Oxytocin,' Eduardo said to Janne, who nodded and administered the injection of the natural hormone that would help the uterus contract and prevent new haemorrhaging.

Eduardo now had the baby out, holding the tiny boy upside down while the nurse who'd been guarding the baby trolley gently sucked mucus out of his mouth and nose.

The little boy gave a cry, and turned a very satisfactory pink colour. The nurse clamped his umbilical cord, held it for Eduardo to cut, then bundled the infant into a warm dry cloth and took him away to check his Agpar score and record the moment of his birth for posterity.

Eduardo delivered the placenta, pointing to the place where it had separated from the wall of the uterus and where the blood had been leaking into the uterine wall, pushing against the foetal sac and disrupting blood supply to the baby.

He checked for more bleeding from the uterus, but as the talking head had said before delivery of the placenta, the problem had resolved itself.

'But she could still need more than ordinary fluid replacement,' the man on the monitor warned. 'And remember there is more danger of post-partum infection after a Caesar than after vaginal deliveries. Especially in this case, where you've had haemorrhaging.'

Eduardo nodded his agreement, his attention focussed on sewing up first the uterus, then the peritoneum, and finally the outer layer of skin. By the time Tess had fitted a drain into the wound and dressed it, Berthe was stirring, and her husband had been invited into Theatre to meet his new son.

Tess stepped out of the way, pulling off her gloves and bloody gown, satisfied yet unable to suppress a tremor of disquiet as she considered what had just occurred. No doubt Berthe's pregnancy had been as trouble-free as her own, right up until the placenta had detached itself from the uterine wall…

Dropping her soiled clothing into a bin, Tess pulled on a clean theatre smock and went back to supervise the theatre clean-up. Although she didn't officially start work until the following day, she knew checking the theatre after use and making sure it was restocked was part of her responsibility.

'It's hardly ever used,' Mathilde had told her, 'so it's not an onerous task. In fact, the islanders are so healthy, days go by without seeing a patient for anything more serious than a pregnancy check-up or a boil to lance.'

So much for that advice, Tess thought as she moved the anaesthetic trolley back against the wall and checked no drugs had been left on it.

'Leave that—you need to eat.'

She'd watched Eduardo leave the theatre, walking beside Berthe as she and the baby had been wheeled away, no doubt to the small ward that served as Tihoroa's hospital. So she was surprised enough by the comment to glance at the clock on the theatre wall—four o'clock already?—before turning to face him.

'This is part of my job,' she reminded him, nodding to the young aide who was holding up the soiled clothes bins prior to removing them to wherever they had to go.

'I would have thought it was also part of your job to look after yourself,' he said, and Tess, suddenly so hungry she felt her stomach cramp, found her anger taking hold again.

But this time she wouldn't give in to it. This time she'd use logic and common sense but still put this man in his place.

'Part of my job to look after myself?' she queried, so softly Eduardo had to look at her to make sure she'd actually spoken. 'And what job is that? Incubator? Brood mare perhaps?'

Smooth, silky words, but with the power to bite into

him. Damn, but the woman was as prickly as the leaves on a breadfruit tree.

But why?

He studied her for a moment, wondering how he could ask about her circumstances, wanting to know more so he could avoid putting his foot into his mouth every time he opened his lips. But before he could think of an offensive way to question her, she spoke again.

'I'm sorry if you have a problem with me being pregnant, but Mathilde has worked in this position through both her pregnancies and not had the slightest hassle or complication. I had assumed you would have seen her example as confirmation I could do the job here. And I can assure you I am quite capable of taking care of myself, without you or anyone else reminding me of the necessity to eat, exercise or get plenty of sleep.'

She smiled at him, a sweet smile but so patently false he wanted to…

Kiss it off her lips?

He couldn't possibly have thought that.

But he had, and the random thought had shaken him so much he nodded abruptly, turned on his heel and walked out of Theatre, striding from the clinic complex and along the path to the lagoon, diving in and swimming strongly back to his island, concentrating on strokes that were automatic to block out the panic his thought had caused.

CHAPTER TWO

THE SCIENTIST IN Eduardo made him list the reasons he'd been attracted to the newcomer.

A fairly lengthy stint of celibacy headed the list. He had felt so devastated by Ilse's behaviour he'd found it hard to regard any woman with equanimity let alone consider attraction towards one of the same species. And though he knew not all women were like Ilse—would *any* other woman have had an affair with the prosecution barrister when her husband had been one of the defendants in a court case?—he'd felt distanced from women since Ilse's betrayal and their subsequent divorce.

Then there was the pregnancy. Not that he was usually attracted to pregnant women, but the fact that Tess *was* pregnant did seem to have awoken all his protective instincts. It was probably some hangover from primitive times, when the survival of the species had depended on men caring for a child-bearer.

He considered adding the long tawny hair, not blonde but a pale brown shot with gold, and the slim body he'd watched as she'd swum, as well as the grey-green eyes she could hide behind thick dark lashes, but decided this would make the list look trivial. Although only having two things on a list made it look pretty trivial as well.

But, attracted or not, he had to work with her. He looked up from his two-item list and shook his head. Talk about distracted! Berthe's little boy had provided a perfectly healthy umbilical cord, and although he'd automatically sealed it in a special plastic bag from the cord kit and popped it into the freezer, he hadn't talked to Berthe and Albert about using it for research. He'd have to go back to the clinic.

And he had to find Tess Beresford and have a proper talk to her—start over again.

With the theatre set back to rights, Janne took Tess to the canteen, explaining as she went, 'It's the company canteen—Tihoroan Pearls—and they own the clinic as well, and although I say "they" I mean we and us because the company belongs to all the people of Tihoroa. Do you understand?'

Tess did understand but only because Mathilde had explained long ago how Eduardo's father had helped the local elders set up a company to grow, harvest and sell the pearls that did so well in the pristine waters around the island group. Every Tihoroan shared in the wealth the pearls brought to the islands, and the company provided not only the clinic but a local school as well, and paid for higher education or training in Australia—and apparently America—for any islander wishing to pursue a career outside the company.

'So in the canteen, as you see,' Janne continued, opening the door and ushering Tess inside, 'there are boatmen and divers and the women who sort the shells and sometimes the specialists who seed the oysters—all different people who are working at the time and need a meal.'

'I can pick out the boatmen, and I guess those three women in bright smocks might be the seeding specialists…'

Janne laughed.

'No, they are our helpers at the clinic. They clean, and take food to patients if anyone is staying in, like Berthe is at the moment. The seeders are those two boys. They have agile fingers and can introduce a little nacre—do you know nacre, mother-of-pearl?—into the oyster. The oyster is irritated by it so it puts protective layers around it and eventually we get a pearl. Ah, here is Eduardo. I will leave him to see you get something to eat and I will organise some food for Berthe and Albert.'

The young nurse turned to Eduardo and spoke rapidly, while tension crept through Tess's body, starting at her toes and worked its way up until she felt as stiff as one of the palm trees under which the canteen sheltered.

'I'm sorry—'

'We seem—'

They spoke together, Tess beginning an apology, the doctor on another tack, but the clash of words made Tess smile, and as her body relaxed she realised the smile was genuine.

'I *am* sorry,' she began, anxious to clear the air between them. 'I shouldn't have spoken to you as I did. I'm afraid I'm a bit over-sensitive about people telling me what to do, even though I know they mean it for the best. But having had my—well, my baby's uncle I suppose you'd call him—nagging me all the way to the airport this morning about my folly in coming here, and my family going on and on about working when I don't need to—it was all just too much.'

Eduardo stared at her, trying to take in the wealth of information she'd just offered him—trying to make sense of what she'd said. But first things first.

He touched her lightly on the shoulder.

'It is I who should be apologising. Mathilde was correct, telling you I worry for other people. I know it can be very irritating and you were right to tell me to back off. Not,' he added with a grin, 'that that will stop me. I will probably continue to annoy you with my worrying.'

Tess smiled and as desire curled inside his abdomen Eduardo wondered if he'd made a big mistake. Being at odds with this woman would have been, undoubtedly, a far better option. For what could he, an emotional refugee, offer any woman…?

'And I'll probably continue to snap at you when you do it,' she agreed, 'but in the meantime, shall we call a truce?'

She moved her hand as if intending to extend it to seal the truce then hesitated slightly before finishing the movement.

Perhaps she'd had second thoughts about the truce, or had she, too, felt something in their earlier contact? Eduardo wondered.

Surely not—she was pregnant with another man's child. The child had an uncle so presumably it also had a father who was away at the moment. She was definitely not available—off limits to other men—and he had to get that into his thick head.

He took her hand and shook it, telling himself to let it go immediately, but somehow he kept hold of it, using it to lead her towards a table by the window where they could look out through hibiscus bushes and fragrant frangipani trees towards the deep blue sea.

'Is it OK to tell you that the coral trout on today's menu is freshly caught and delicious, if you fancy fish? Or am I being too officious again?' he said lightly, hoping to see her smile break out again.

Tess knew he was teasing her, and didn't like how it made her feel—kind of warm and happy and excited all at the same time. But he looked so anxious she had to smile.

'I haven't been eating much seafood because of mercury levels in our fish at home and concern for the baby, but I'm guessing the fish up here don't know about mercury.'

His answering smile made her feel warmer and even more excited—well, not excited so much as internally jumpy—and while she was considering this phenomenon he announced he'd get her the best piece of fish on Tihoroa and walked away.

She looked around, thinking she could be in a company canteen anywhere in the world, except here the dress was definitely casual, and the soft, musical voices of the islanders was a kinder background noise than piped music. But once she looked outside, the unreality of her situation hit her. She really *was* on a tropical island in the Pacific Ocean, with no concerns except doing a good job at the clinic and regaining her peace of mind and confidence about the path she'd chosen. She looked at the serenity of the blue sea, and knew she'd made the right decision. Here, without any outside pressure, she could set aside her doubts and uncertainties about single motherhood, and be ready to face the birth of her baby with the same determination that had led to her decision to have Grant's child.

'So, your family do not approve of your coming here?'

Tess was so startled by this opening salvo from Eduardo as he put a tray down on the table she felt her mouth drop open.

'Didn't we just shake on a truce to stay off personal issues?' she asked, although she couldn't feel angry right now when her mouth was filling with saliva as the aroma of the meals on the tray reached her taste buds.

'Not a bit of it,' he replied, setting a plate with a lightly grilled piece of fish in front of her, then offering a bowl of salad that had a tang of coconut about it. 'We shook on an agreement that I'd probably keep annoying you by caring for your welfare and you'd probably keep snapping at me for doing it, but you can't drop a little snippet of information like the baby's uncle nagging you and your family wanting you to stop work, and not expect me to ask questions.'

'I can't?' Tess teased, flaking a piece of fish off onto her fork and raising it to her lips. 'Oh, this is heavenly. I could smell coconut and thought it was in the salad, but it's on the fish, isn't it?'

Eduardo shook his head. From the way Tess was attacking her meal, he'd get no sense from her until her appetite was satisfied. Although watching her enjoy the simple food he himself enjoyed was special somehow, which was the last thing he should be thinking. Given the unexpected attraction he'd felt earlier, the less he had to do with this woman, the better.

But she was so wholehearted in her pleasure, forking flakes of the succulent white flesh into her mouth, her eyes smiling her delight, he couldn't help but watch her.

'Want some of mine?' he offered, when her piece of fish had all but disappeared.

'Definitely not! That was far too much for me as it was, but I just couldn't stop eating it. I'd better have some salad now so the baby gets its greens, and I'd better work out an exercise programme because if I keep eating this much at a meal I'll be the size of a house by the time I go home.'

'Which brings us neatly back to the question you didn't answer. Just what kind of pressure did you leave at home that my asking you questions was so upsetting?'

Tess pushed herself back from the table with a satisfied sigh, then studied the man across the table. OK, so she found him attractive, but that was understandable as a woman would have to be dead *not* to find him attractive. It wasn't just his looks, but an air of—was it danger?—that hung about him. Or maybe it was power, leashed but ready to explode.

But the issue here wasn't attraction, however it might manifest itself, the issue here was work. For the next four weeks they would be colleagues so it was only natural he would want to know something of her background.

'Mathilde didn't tell you?'

He shook his head and he, too pushed back from the table, folding his arms across his chest with the air of a man for whom time had no limits.

Which it probably didn't, here where there were no trains to catch, no commuting to do.

'She told me your name and your qualifications, which is all I was required to know. I suppose that's why I was startled to find you were pregnant.'

Tess nodded, understanding how he must have felt, understanding too that he might be feeling let down by Mathilde—blaming her for arranging what he obviously saw as an unsatisfactory replacement.

But where to start?

With Mathilde—to let her off the hook first.

'Don't blame Mathilde,' Tess began. 'When she told me

she was coming to the mainland I begged to be allowed to take her place. My pregnancy has been textbook perfect so I knew I'd be OK, and I really needed to get away for a while. And the timing was perfect. I could fill in for her and be home in time for Christmas, which was when I intended to stop work to prepare for the new arrival.'

Dark eyes scanned her face, as if trying to see beneath her skin.

'You needed to get away? From whom? Your family? The baby's uncle?'

Tess sighed.

'From him, and my parents, and a few well-meaning friends.' She leaned forward, rested her elbows on the table and propped her chin on her hands. 'The biggest decision I've ever made in my life was to have this baby,' she began, studying Eduardo's face in the hope she'd see some sympathy there. 'But you have to go back nearly fourteen years to understand. I was eighteen, a very sheltered eighteen, an only child, with family money, engaged to be married to the boy next door, the only boy I'd ever loved. He was diagnosed with a very aggressive leukaemia three months before the wedding, and before beginning radiotherapy and chemo the specialist suggested we freeze some of his sperm in case...'

Eduardo shook his head as if hearing her story caused him hurt, but now she was launched into the telling, she had to keep going.

'You'd know about the "in case" scenario—about sterility following treatment—but with Grant there was no future at all, as he died six months later.'

No tears—they were long gone—but the sadness had stayed like a bruise on her heart and she pressed one hand against it now as she continued.

'Being with him through his treatment shook me out of my sheltered little world and made me grow up. After he died, I started training as a nurse and for the first time in my life I realised what independence was all about. It wasn't an easy way to grow up—to lose a loved one—but I liked the person I became and I loved nursing and suddenly I had another kind of life. Not the one I'd thought I'd have but one I really enjoyed and found fulfilling.'

'Until twenty-seven weeks ago?'

She smiled at the grave-faced man who'd asked the question.

'It was a little longer ago than that,' she admitted. 'I loved my job but I wasn't totally and wholeheartedly committed to it as the sole purpose in my life. I thought, as the pain of Grant's death faded, I'd meet someone else, fall in love, marry and have children. But it didn't happen, Eduardo, and then one day I'd been thinking about Grant and remembering just how nice a person he had been, and I thought it unfair that nothing of him remained...'

'Except some frozen sperm,' Eduardo offered, and Tess nodded.

'I'm thirty-two,' she said defensively. 'This wasn't just a whim. I thought it through and wrote down all the pros and cons and set out a financial plan whereby I could take time off work to care for a baby for a few years then work part time while he or she was at school.'

Eduardo heard the defensiveness in her voice and guessed her decision hadn't seemed nearly as sensible to her friends and family.

Why?

'Did your parents not want a grandchild?'

Tess smiled at him—but it was a smile tinged with

sadness, so much so he found himself hoping she'd never smile like that again.

'Oh, they wanted a grandchild—they thought it a wonderful idea, the best ever. I'm an only child, you see, and having a grandchild for them was on my list of pros when I made the decision, but—'

What had she said earlier? Family money?

'They wanted to take over? They wanted you to come home and be cosseted and cared for and fussed over.' Eduardo shook his head at these guesses. 'I've known you less than a day and already I know that would not sit well with you. It must have seemed to you that they had never accepted the person you'd grown into. That to them you were still the young eighteen-year-old about to marry the boy next door.'

'Exactly,' Tess said, no sadness in the smile this time. In fact, it held delight, as if finally she'd found someone who understood. 'And Dan, Grant's brother, was the same, enthusiastic and delighted, but—'

She stopped abruptly, leaving Eduardo with the impression that the baby's uncle might have had concerns she didn't want to voice, but before he could press her for an answer, she was speaking again.

'Sometimes it seemed as if the world was ranged against me—but worst of all, it was ranged in the name of love— for love—because they do all love me.'

Eduardo heard the words but heard more than words— he heard despair tinged with uncertainty, which was strange, given that she must have worked through all her doubts before deciding to get pregnant, and his first impressions of her had been of a strong, capable woman well able to take care of herself. He studied her, now tackling the salad—giving her baby some greens.

So what had thrown her so much she'd escaped to an island in the middle of nowhere? Had it just been family pressure offered in the name of love?

Or was she having doubts about the decision she'd taken?

Was she having doubts about her ability to bring up a baby on her own?

Ideally, a baby should have two parents, and everyone needed someone to love and be loved by…

Everyone but him?

Nonsense! His situation was entirely different. Here on Tihoroa he was emotionally safe. He had all the islanders to love and be loved by, and he wasn't seven months pregnant…

But he could hardly tell her his thoughts, or add his voice to those of her family, especially when he remembered the despair and uncertainty he'd heard as she'd spoken. He reached out across the table and took her hand.

'You have had to put up with this emotional pressure right through your pregnancy?' he asked, wondering how she'd managed to resist this most insidious kind of love for seven months.

Tess shook her head. What she should do was remove her hand from under Eduardo's but it felt comfortable there—warm and somehow safe—so she left it where it was and continued her saga.

'I didn't tell them until I was starting to show, which was only at about eighteen weeks, not because I expected
them to react the way they did—although I should have guessed—but because I didn't want anyone getting excited until I knew for sure I'd carry the baby full term and nothing much could go wrong.'

In saying the words, she must have betrayed the niggle of disquiet that she'd felt earlier because Eduardo's fingers tightened on hers.

'Abruptio placentae is very rare,' he said quietly, and she shook her head in amazement.

'How—?'

'It would have been unnatural for you not to feel some concern, having seen Berthe in trouble today,' he said, his thumb rubbing against hers on the table.

Could such a gesture—the slide of skin on skin—cause tremors far more disquieting than her concern for her unborn child?

What was happening to her?

She'd come in search of tranquillity, not added complications.

Very carefully, Tess slid her hand out from under his, using it to stack their plates together.

'Speaking of which, I should go and check on Berthe and the baby,' she said and stood up, needing to get away from not so much the man as the emotional disturbances he was causing.

'I'm going over to the clinic myself. We'll go together and I can show you around.'

No escape, but in a funny way she wasn't displeased— in fact, she was enjoying this man's company, which was very strange as her most common reaction to men was to feel wary, knowing they might want more of her than she was prepared to give, especially early in any relationship.

Perhaps, she decided, following Eduardo out into the gathering dusk, pregnancy was providing her with a kind of armour. No man could be interested in a seven-months-pregnant woman so, being safe from the kind of attentions she had always found unsettling, she could relax and enjoy his company.

'We will watch the sunset before we go inside?'

It was a question but he obviously expected her agreement, for he touched his hand to her shoulder and guided her to where a fallen palm provided a place to sit at the edge of the sand. Further along the beach she could see movement on the clinic veranda.

'Berthe, showing her new son the sunset,' Eduardo said, as Tess realised one of the onlookers was in a wheelchair. 'Many of the islanders stop what they are doing to take in the wonder of the end of day.'

And as Tess watched the colours in the sky deepen from the faintest pink to scarlet and vermilion and the reflections of the vibrant colours light the placid sea, she understood why they took the time.

'I am glad I came,' she said quietly, when the colours had faded and the sky had turned a deep blue. 'Nothing puts things back into perspective as easily as one of nature's many wonderful displays.'

Eduardo didn't answer. Was he thinking about the upheavals he'd had in his life and the wounds he'd suffered? Had they been too strong and too deep for even the beauty of nature to heal? And would he talk about it? Would talking about them help him?

It had certainly helped her. She felt calmer and more at ease than she had for weeks.

She studied his profile for a while, respecting his silence yet wanting to know more of him—wanting him to talk…

He stood up and she followed, walking with him towards the clinic, wondering whether there was a key to open up Eduardo del Riga as easily as he'd opened her up.

As they approached the clinic a small child broke away from the group and ran towards them.

''Duardo!' he cried, holding up his arms with confident expectation.

And he wasn't disappointed. Eduardo grasped the little boy under his arms and swung him high in the air, then turned him into a plane and zoomed him high and low, before settling him astride his broad shoulders.

'Good thing he hasn't had his dinner yet,' Albert re- marked, but Tess had been watching Eduardo's face and had seen the uncomplicated delight and affection in it. Were children—even babies—the key?

And *why* was she so intrigued?

Why did she want this man to talk to her?

They were colleagues, but she guessed she'd see little of him outside work, and in four weeks she'd be gone…

She'd paused in the shadows as he'd lifted the little boy and now watched as he set him down, then bent to lift the baby from Berthe's arms, turning towards Albert as he held the newborn. Albert beamed with pride in response to whatever comment Eduardo had made.

Was she wrong, Tess wondered, denying her baby a father? *Should* she marry Dan?

She sighed, frustrated that her thoughts had taken such a turn. She was here to reaffirm her original decision—to take the path of single motherhood—so why, away from all outside influence and pressure, was she raising doubts of her own?

Because a man had tossed a small boy in the air?

She must be more tired than she'd realised. Although it

was still early, she'd had a long day. She'd check on Berthe and the baby, ask someone how she would be contacted if she was needed during the night, then go to bed.

But checking on Berthe and the baby meant joining Eduardo in that family group and although she was sure she'd mentally settled the fact that he was nothing more than a kind colleague, and that whatever she might feel in the way of attraction was to do with her rampant hormones, the fact that her body kept responding to his made her feet feel heavy as she moved towards them.

'You will see the little one is doing well, but Berthe should be back in bed,' Eduardo greeted her. 'And this is Philippe, who will be their nurse tonight.'

Tess held out her hand to the young islander.

'Philippe is from one of the outer islands in the group,' Eduardo explained. 'He will be returning there for his days off when we go later in the week. Albert will be with us also as he's the clinic boatman.'

'Like an ambulance driver back home?' Tess suggested, forgetting her reluctance to be close to Eduardo as she considered this new way of life into which she'd plunged.

'Not really,' Albert told her, 'although the boat is kitted out with all the stuff you find in an ambulance, but my training is as a sailor so I need a nurse or doctor on any of my runs. Not that we have many emergencies. We islanders are tough and healthy.'

He waved a hand towards the three children pressed close to their mother, and Tess understood his pride. She also felt a surge of quite different excitement. One day she could be the nurse going on the boat with Albert. She'd certainly be doing trips to other islands to hold clinics there.

'You are a woman who likes a challenge, I think,' Eduardo said, as Berthe was wheeled back to her room and her family followed. 'I saw excitement in your eyes as Albert talked of his work.'

Tess shook her head in disbelief.

'That's the second time you've picked up on my thoughts. Am I really so easy to read?' she asked.

He smiled at her, and she knew the shivers of attraction would continue to plague her no matter how often her head reminded her he was nothing but a colleague.

'I too love the island visits and the variety of work I do here, so it was easy to understand your reaction,' Eduardo told her, then, seeing her frown, added, 'You don't believe me?'

'I don't disbelieve you but wonder that you don't feel the need to be more challenged. Coming here is a challenge for me, but for you—more of an escape, surely?'

Eduardo's first reaction was resentment—that she would put into words the dissatisfaction he'd been feeling lately. True, he had his research, but in spite of all the modern marvels of technology and his internet links to laboratories around the world, he knew he needed the mental stimulus of talking with his fellow researchers and—she was right—more challenges.

But he didn't have to admit it. This woman was already disturbing him in a way he didn't like. To talk to her—really talk—would draw them closer and that was the last thing he needed. Her future was back on the mainland with the families of her child around to support her. His future? Well, he still had no idea what his future held or even what he wanted it to hold...

'My returning here *was* an escape,' he said slowly,

choosing each word with care so he didn't reveal just how emotionally spent he'd been when he'd returned to Tihoroa. 'But why should it not now be a lifestyle choice? All over the world people are making changes, moving to a slower-paced way of life. Why not me?'

She smiled again and shook her head.

'I can't see it,' she said, then she walked away, following the route Berthe and her family had taken into the clinic, leaving him with a tangle of unsettled thoughts.

Tess watched as Philippe settled Berthe back into bed. Eduardo hadn't followed them into the room, so maybe the tour of the clinic could take place some other time.

Not that she'd mind—she was suddenly very, very tired.

'I will phone you if I need you,' Philippe assured her as she said goodnight to him outside Berthe's room.

'Not tonight, Philippe. Phone me instead.'

Tess turned to see Eduardo leaning against the wall of the corridor. As he met her eyes he held up his hands in a classic sign of surrender.

'Don't attack me again. You can take my on-call night later in the week, although it's rare anyone is called out at night.'

'Just as long as I do take it,' Tess told him, trying to sound sincere but so grateful she could have hugged him.

He had a strong, muscled body—it would be good to hug…

Startled not by the thought but by the physical ache it caused in her arms, she hurried on, 'And if you wouldn't mind, I'd like to leave the clinic tour until tomorrow. I'm pooped!'

He smiled at her and shook his head.

'Teetering on exhaustion, I would say,' he teased, 'if you actually admit to being tired. Come on, I'll walk you home.'

Tess opened her mouth to argue then closed it again. Walking under the palm trees with this man might just be the perfect end to a very unusual day.

Although to even think such a thing proved she'd lost her mind!

CHAPTER THREE

SHE WOKE UP WITH a sense of disorientation so complete she had to sit up and look around at the white-painted floor, the woven walls, the thick beams that held up the thatched roof of her hut.

'Tihoroa,' she whispered to herself, then, suddenly excited by all that lay ahead of her, she leapt out of bed, had a quick wash, pulled on her bikini and shirt and headed for the deserted lagoon she'd discovered the previous day.

It was just after six so she had plenty of time for a swim before breakfast—presumably at the canteen—after which she'd get an early start on exploring the clinic. Preferably early enough to avoid Eduardo.

She shivered and tugged her shirt more tightly around her body, although the shiver had nothing to do with the cool morning air. The shiver was reaction to even thinking of the man who'd walked her home the previous evening, beside her but not touching her—close enough for her body to be crying out for even an accidental brush of his arm against hers, or his hip against her hip.

By the time they'd reached the hut, she'd been so twitchy she'd mumbled a hurried goodnight and escaped into the darkness, only realising, once he'd departed, that she had no idea where the light switches were, or even if the hut had lights.

Finding the light switches had been easy. It had been trying to analyse her reaction to Eduardo that had kept her mind occupied until the deep, almost drugged sleep of a healthy tiredness had claimed her.

It *had* to be the pregnancy issue, something to do with her present hormone balance—or imbalance. She and Grant had shared a physical attraction but, thinking back, she couldn't remember it being as strong as the way Eduardo made her feel. And she'd dated countless other men, kissed more than a few of them—even wanted to feel attraction to one or two of them—but had never felt the slightest tremor.

So why else, apart from pregnancy, would her body be positively humming with desire whenever she was near Eduardo del Riga?

She reached the beach, stripped off her shirt and splashed through the shallows, shivering slightly as the cool water swirled around her legs.

If she concentrated on work, and on staying fit, doing her exercises and preparing both her body and her mind for the arrival of the baby, surely she'd be able to block out the very inconvenient desire she was feeling for Eduardo.

Avoiding him as much as possible would make it easier.

Hadn't Mathilde said he rarely visited the clinic more than once a day, and sometimes not even then if he wasn't needed. Before his return to Tihoroa, the island hadn't had a doctor, just the small clinic staffed by nurses, with access to the Australian flying doctors should they be needed.

However, Eduardo *was* a doctor, and he was here, so he'd probably feel he had to keep an eye on his temporary supervisor…

Startled to find that particular thought excited more than angered her, she slowly eased the rest of her body into the clear water and began to swim. There was a small rocky island on the far side of the lagoon. She'd explore it one day. Enough for now to swim then get ready for the day.

The splash in the water not far from where she swam made her think of sharks and panic seized her, then she remembered Mathilde telling her the lagoon was fringed by coral reefs which kept out not only sharks and stingrays but bigger fish as well. But an atavistic fear kept her still—well, as still as she could be while treading water in order not to drown. Then she saw the dark head break the surface of the water and there was Eduardo, not only reading her fear but grinning at her.

'How could you do that to me?' she yelled at him, fury following relief so closely she didn't think to choose her words. 'I thought it was a shark. I could have had a heart attack and died.'

Totally unrepentant, he continued to smile, while stroking lazily towards her.

'There are no sharks in the lagoon—the reef keeps them out—but if you had had a heart attack I could have revived you, shown you my prowess with mouth-to-mouth resuscitation.'

He was teasing her—half-flirting as he probably half-flirted with every woman who crossed his path, Tess realised, but that didn't stop her heart leaping around in her chest at the thought of Eduardo's lips pressed to hers.

She backed away from him, angry now at herself.

'Mathilde said no one used this lagoon—that everyone swam at the beach near the clinic.'

'Everyone but me. It is partly out of respect for my family that the islanders don't use the lagoon.' He nodded towards the island she had yet to explore. 'That is my home, and they like to give me my privacy.'

Uh-oh! He might be smiling—pirates probably smiled as they forced their victims at sword point along the plank—but he'd swum out here to give her a warning, to make it clear this was his territory. So she wouldn't be swimming here again *or* exploring the little island, but disappointment gave way to intrigue as she remembered his wet shorts the previous day.

'And you swim across to work each day? Well, that makes a train commute seem very ordinary.'

To her surprise, he laughed, so joyous a sound Tess's heart began its misbehaviour all over again.

'I come around the coast by boat or jet ski usually. My jetty is on the other side of the island, and it takes no longer than five minutes from my place to the clinic.'

'Taking a jet ski to work!' Tess shook her head in amazement. 'City folk don't know what they're missing.'

'You're right there,' he agreed, but the good humour was gone from his voice and she wondered if he was thinking back to the conversation they'd had the previous evening when she'd challenged him about being satisfied working here.

What a choice to have to make—to leave this paradise for the city, and for what? The betterment of mankind? It sounded noble, put like that, but she knew the hours researchers put into their work, more often than not proving their theories wrong and having to start all over again, frustration heaped on frustration.

And after the court case, where he and his fellow researchers had been falsely accused of ethical misconduct—by a woman, according to Mathilde, whose advances he'd spurned—would he ever want to return to that life?

'Would you ever go back?' she asked, uncertain why she'd felt the need to blurt out her question right here and now.

'I don't know,' he said, his dark eyes clouded with pain. Or was she imagining pain—perhaps the clouds were nothing more than the indecision he was admitting to? 'I honestly don't know.'

He ducked his head in a kind of nod to her and swam away, returning to his island. And now she knew it was private, she could hardly follow.

Disappointment accompanied her back to the beach, although whether it was disappointment that she hadn't learned more about Eduardo, or disappointment that he hadn't spent more time with her, she couldn't decide.

Neither could she decide which reason would be more acceptable to her.

Time to think of other things—time for breakfast then off to work!

The sight of fresh chopped fruit, pawpaw, mango, banana and slices of coconut, all laid out on banana leaves in the servery at the canteen distracted her from thoughts of Eduardo and she helped herself to a bowlful, added some yoghurt, poured a glass of juice and, not wanting to intrude on the islander groups, found herself an empty table.

Philippe soon joined her.

'Now, that's what I call a real man's breakfast,' Tess said, nodding to his plate laden with sausages, eggs, bacon, beans and toast.

'You get very hungry here by the sea,' he told her. 'That's a medical fact.'

His face split in a huge grin.

'Or if it isn't, it should be. Eduardo, he keeps asking the canteen to stop offering what he calls cholesterol-challenge type of breakfasts, but we islanders have grown up with big breakfasts—our traditional breakfast is a kind of porridge but with fish and seafood—so switching to this kind of breakfast was easy. And anyway, Eduardo eats the sweet buns and croissants the chefs make, which are much more laden with fats than my sausages. It is his European heritage, I suppose.'

He likes sweet buns—Tess tucked this scrap of information away as carefully as she would a precious gem, then chided herself for being stupid. Eduardo meant nothing to her. She was here to escape relationship muddles while he, single, wealthy, good-looking and sexy as hell, could choose from just about any woman anywhere in the world—should he want a woman, that was. But the chiding didn't take, for the next minute she was asking Philippe for more information.

'You talk of European heritage—Mathilde told me Portuguese sailors made their homes on the islands hundreds of years ago.'

'Portuguese and some French as well—we call them sailors but they were probably pirates. They took island women as their wives so all of us have some European blood by now. Eduardo's people were different. His family have always been master jewellers back in Portugal, making rich, special pieces for the royal family, among others, and they came here for the pearls. They bought their land from the traditional owners, and they have always worked for the betterment of the islanders. They also kept their links to their homeland because that's where their business is, so they educated their children in Portugal, although Eduardo later studied medicine in Australia.'

More snippets to tuck away.

How pathetic was this?

She finished her breakfast, said goodbye to Philippe and headed for the clinic, a weak cup of coffee—one of two she allowed herself each day—held in one hand.

'Coffee when you're pregnant?'

So much for not seeing much of Eduardo. It was only a little after seven and this was already her second encounter of the day with him.

'Don't start,' she warned him. 'It's very weak but it smelt so delicious I couldn't resist. You'd never get coffee like this in a hospital canteen.'

He smiled his agreement and she remembered all the reasons she was hoping to not see much of him while she was there.

'Going over to the clinic? Hoping to get a head start on the day?'

It was her turn to smile, although she knew exchanging smiles was nearly as dangerous as touching him.

'Hoping to be able to find my way around the place before the first patient arrives. I also want to check on Berthe and the baby. The specialist's warning about infection is prodding away at my mind.'

'I've checked—no temperature—and the baby is feeding well already so I suspect Berthe's dates may have been a bit out and he's not as premmie as we thought.'

'I wondered about that when he was born—he was so big—but then I thought maybe big babies were the norm here.'

'Big healthy babies,' Eduardo said, shooting a teasing glance at her coffee.

'Two a day! That's all I have,' Tess snapped at him. '*And* the occasional glass of wine now and then if I feel like it.'

She felt like adding 'so there' and maybe putting her thumb on her nose and waggling her fingers at him, but realised that would be behaving exactly like the child her parents still thought her so she muttered something that might have been goodbye and marched away instead—sipping her coffee, which now tasted like diluted mud.

She'd have thrown it away only she was reasonably sure Eduardo was watching her and she didn't want him to know he'd won.

But once inside the clinic all her tetchiness vanished. The place was a delight. It was built so every habitable room looked out towards the sea, with treatment rooms, the theatre and storerooms tucked away on the landward side.

Having satisfied herself she'd be able to find most things she might need, she visited Berthe who was anxious to get home to her family but understood she had to give her wound time to heal.

'I don't trust that Albert to give the kids good food,' she said, handing the new baby to Tess to hold while she shifted from her bed to a wheelchair.

The infant had just been fed, and his milky lips were pursed into a pink bud. The sight of this, the dark eyes looking intently into hers, the feel of the small body securely wrapped, all combined to start flutters in Tess's heart. Not Eduardo flutters, but new-baby flutters. Soon she'd be holding *her* baby. Grant's baby!

All at once the feelings she was experiencing when near Eduardo seemed a betrayal of the man whose child she carried. Sunny, open, good-hearted and a friend to everyone—that was how Grant had been. Nice! It seemed such a feeble word, but it covered everything she'd known about him. And her belief that there should be more people like Grant in the world had been at the top of her list when she'd decided to have his baby.

As for Eduardo—she didn't know him well, but she wasn't certain 'nice' would fit. Oh, he could play nice easily enough—he'd done just that in the lagoon this morning while at the same time warning her off. Playing nice was part of his charm, but could men with the dangerous allure that floated around him ever be called nice?

Neither was she certain she could control her reactions to the man, which brought her back to the odd feeling of betrayal. The best thing would be to avoid him as much as possible, and that's the course she took, taking breaks in the canteen at odd hours, even finding a village shop that sold fresh fruit and bread and other basic provisions so she could make some meals for herself and avoid the canteen altogether.

Her clinic hours were divided into sessions, so one morning she might be checking and vaccinating babies and the next talking to geriatrics about good nutrition.

'The canteen provides meals for a lot of the older people,' Janne explained, the day a group of elderly patients had been delivered to the clinic by the school bus. 'Like your Meals-on-Wheels on the mainland. But often they don't eat the meals straight away, and the food can spoil so we have to work out a better way of doing this.'

Tess kept this in mind as she examined the patients. Tropical ulcers were common, as the tissue-thin skin on legs particularly was easily torn and the wound difficult to heal.

'Manuka honey is being used a lot for leg ulcers at home,' she told Janne, as they bathed a particularly nasty ulcer.

'My mother used honey—not with a fancy name, but she put honey on everything,' the patient said. 'I forgot that until you said it. I have honey at home. I'll use that.'

He stood up but Tess urged him back into his seat, not at all certain of the properties or the sterile qualities of local honey.

'We'll try this antibiotic first,' she suggested. 'And dress it again. Can you keep it dry?'

The old man shook his head.

'Keeping it dry is no good. You have to go into the sea each day with sores like this. That is another way to cure it.'

'You've been doing that for two months and the ulcer is growing,' Janne reminded him. 'Now it's time to try our way, or you'll have to come into hospital so we can make sure you keep it dry.'

He glared at her but Tess guessed the threat of hospital might keep him out of the water for a few days at least. And in the meantime she'd order some medicinal honey to be sent up on the weekly supply plane.

Her next patient was a huge woman with unstable diabetes.

'We're trying to control Marianne's diabetes with diet,' Janne explained as the woman settled carefully into a chair then lifted her bare feet onto the desk.

'My diet's good—I'm keeping to it,' Marianne informed Tess. 'It is my feet you need to check because that's what I'm not so good at. Can't reach the damn things!'

Marianne's vast bulk shook with laughter, but Tess, mentally running through foot care for diabetic patients, realised she was speaking the truth.

'Three times a week—that's when you do my feet. But

Janne can do them if you like. Mathilde, she just likes to look first.'

Tess eyed the large, calloused feet resting on her desk and decided she, too, should have a look first.

Although Marianne's legs were scaly, Tess could find no blisters, or signs of itching, or dry cracked skin on Marianne's feet. There was slight swelling and blueness around the veins but nothing that was of concern.

'They're looking good,' she told the patient, who beamed at her.

'That's my Tomas,' Marianne said proudly. 'He checks them for me and dries between my toes the way the nurses say, and puts on cream.'

'Tomas is your husband?' Tess guessed, and brought forth more laughter from Marianne.

'He's my great-grandson—a good boy. Eduardo says he can be a doctor later on.'

Great-grandson? The woman looked about fifty.

'I'm sixty-eight,' Marianne said proudly, but while Tess was amazed that she'd been so far out in her estimate, she was also concerned. Perhaps all the people of Tihoroa could read minds. Either that, or her face betrayed her every passing thought.

Marianne went off with Janne to have her feet soaked, her nails cut, calluses removed and lanolin rubbed gently into her legs and feet. Young Tomas was obviously doing a great job but some things were still beyond him.

'I am Rose, Mathilde's grandmother,' the next elderly patient announced. 'I've brought presents for your baby.'

Rose handed Tess a parcel and, unwrapping it, she found a woven basket filled with shells. Beautiful shells, some so pale and fragile looking she wondered how they'd survived a passage through the reef, while others were bright with colour.

'This one,' Rose continued, picking up what Tess knew to be a baler, 'is so the child can hold it to her ear and will always be able to hear the sea.'

'*Her* ear?' Tess queried, and the woman nodded and smiled.

'You're carrying a girl. I was the baby woman on these islands for many years—what you would call a midwife. My mother was the same before me, but my daughter became a teacher and Mathilde, she carries on the tradition but with new methods.'

Rose didn't seem put out about new methods, probably realising the changes would basically be in the drugs available, because babies had always arrived the same way.

'Now, you're here for an appointment?' Tess asked, when she'd thanked Rose for the gift.

'No, I come to give you the shells and to have a look at you. A lot of the people on the bus today are here to have a look at you. We hear you have no husband. What a pity that Eduardo is being so stubborn about not marrying again and so stupid about not trusting all women because of the perfidy of two of them. But for you, perhaps a marriage of convenience, as they call them in the love stories I read. Arranged marriages have worked all through the ages, and all babies need a father.'

Tess shook her head, unable to believe what she was hearing. First the announcement that the child she carried was a girl—how could Rose possibly know that for certain?

And now this talk about a husband—with Eduardo mentioned in the same breath. How ridiculous! Even more ridiculous was the tiny bounce of excitement Tess had felt in her chest!

Get over it, girl! If you want a husband there's a perfectly good candidate waiting for you back on the mainland.

But Rose had sounded so genuinely interested in Tess's well-being she couldn't get annoyed.

'I've plenty of people telling me the same thing back home,' she said. 'Not about marrying Eduardo but about finding a father for my baby, but women through the ages have also been widowed and managed to bring up their children on their own. In an island country like this you would know of accidents that happen. Women can do anything.'

Rose nodded her agreement, then she shot a teasing smile at Tess. 'Except give themselves more babies, or put their arms around themselves. Remember that.'

And suddenly Tess remembered how she'd longed for Eduardo's touch the previous evening. Was Rose right? Did women need strong arms around them now and then in order to be complete?

Impossible!

She was showing Rose out of the office when the man in question appeared.

'Rose! How are you? Checking out the opposition, are you?'

He put his arms around the older woman and gave her a huge hug.

Help! If people weren't reading her thoughts, they were acting them out in front of her!

But Eduardo didn't stay to distract her yet again, escorting Rose out of the room then, as Tess watched, walking away from the clinic and towards the canteen.

'Did he want something?' Tess asked Janne, nodding in the direction the pair were taking.

'Just to see Rose. He must have guessed she'd come in to see you. A lot of the islanders, they only come if something special's happening. Rose was his nanny when he was little—and I think maybe his father's as well.'

More bits of jigsaw to add to her picture of Eduardo…

She didn't see him again that day, although late on Wednesday afternoon he appeared as she was sitting with Berthe, listening to the various ways her older children had arrived in the world.

'Berthe telling you about the baby that arrived in the boat?' he said, propping herself in the doorway and leaning negligently there, so relaxed—so at ease—Tess couldn't believe the tension he was causing in *her* body.

'We did that one earlier—she's just been telling me about number three, who came while she was swimming one day.'

'He's still my little fish,' Berthe told her. 'Two years old and swims better than the big children.'

Tess remembered the little boy who'd raced towards Eduardo, confident of being swung up into his strong arms. Maybe Eduardo *was* nice!

She glanced at him as he examined Berthe's wound and shook her head. 'Nice' was far too placid—too safe—a word for Eduardo. There was nothing safe about a man who could trip her pulse with a glance, and send shivers down her spine with a touch.

'Tomorrow,' he said to Berthe, 'you can go home but Albert will be with us on the clinic run so I have asked Rose to stay with you and mind the other children. You can supervise and watch them at play, but you're not to move around too much, understand?'

Berthe beamed at him. 'That is good, Eduardo. I'll behave, you'll see, and with Rose there the children will all be little angels.'

'I'm sure,' Eduardo said drily, winking at Tess as he spoke.

'That's about as likely as the coconut palms bearing bananas—wilder children than Berthe's I've yet to meet,' he told her as they walked away. 'She's too soft-hearted to chastise them, and with Albert away a lot she's the main influence.'

'But they're much loved,' Tess said, having seen the affection both parents lavished on the children. 'Surely that's the most important thing.'

'In the end, yes,' Eduardo agreed, 'although, as you've discovered, love itself can sometimes be a tyranny.'

Tess didn't answer, too aware of him—too bemused by his understanding of her dilemma. They had reached the clinic's reception area and he nodded towards a small pile of files already zipped into a thick plastic envelope.

'Ah, you've remembered tomorrow is the clinic run to the outer islands,' he said.

'Actually, Janne remembered. She's the one who found the files we'll need and showed me the equipment we take,' Tess admitted, then, remembering something else Janne had told her, she added, 'But you don't always do the clinic run. Are you intending to go tomorrow or just checking I have everything organised?'

Eduardo turned away from the files and seemed to study her for a moment before answering.

'I'll be with you tomorrow,' he said, and although it was a very normal kind of statement, it sent alarm rattling along

Tess's nerves. 'To introduce you to the people, and to show you around the islands.'

He spoke with such pride Tess felt stupid for reacting as she had. She meant nothing more to him than any other guest worker would, and his politeness—niceness—was to her as a colleague, not a woman.

'Now it is late, I'll walk you home.'

Politeness, she reminded herself again, but from her side it was far too dangerous to be walking in moonlight, beneath palm trees, with the gentle soughing of the sea against the coral beach and the sexiest man she'd ever met by her side.

This was the danger she'd sensed in him from the start...

'I'll be fine. I find my way back and forth to my little home all the time now,' she said, through lips dry from the private admission that she found him sexy.

'I'll walk you home,' he repeated, and she knew, no matter what she said, he'd do just that.

Torture, that's what it was. Walking beside him along the path of broken coral pieces, bleached white by the sun. To sidetrack thoughts she didn't want to think, she did a check of her body. Legs felt good and when she'd prodded her ankles earlier there'd been no sign of swelling. Back OK. She rubbed at the place in the small of it where aches began if she was on her feet too long. The ache had stayed today but once she was—

'Your back is aching?'

Eduardo had seen her hand move to rub the base of her spine. What was wrong with him that he was thinking of his own reactions to this woman—thinking lustful thoughts, in fact—when he should be thinking of her health and welfare?

'Just a little,' she murmured, as if not wanting to spoil the quiet of the night. 'It happens when I'm on my feet a lot—it's quite natural and will go once I shower and get into bed.'

Images of her naked under the shower, water sliding off her lush body, popped obligingly into his head and he cursed the fact that his libido had suddenly stirred back to life. This woman was a colleague, here for only four weeks, and they had to work together...

'Come into the hut and I will rub it for you,' he said, then did a mental scan to check his motives. Definitely pure—she was a colleague and this was a medical matter, nothing more.

So why did his mouth feel dry?

Inwardly he groaned, but once inside the hut he was all business.

'Sit astride this chair,' he told his patient, pulling out a straight-backed chair from the small writing desk in one corner of the room. 'Rest your forearms on the back of it and your head on your arms. Will you take off your shirt or would you prefer me just to pull it up?'

Take the second option, he begged silently, but she hesitated, then with a sigh sat down, pulled her shirt over her head and dragged her heavy swathe of hair forward over one shoulder.

Glimpses of full breasts and the beguiling swell of her pregnant belly, but from behind all he saw was a pale-skinned back, curving inward at the waist then swelling out to shapely hips.

'I'll be a moment,' he said, and went into the bathroom, mostly to wash his hands but also to give himself a small lecture on self-control. That done, he searched among the toiletries supplied to all the guest huts, finding what he wanted in a small, red-topped jar.

'Whipped coconut oil with a hint of chilli for heat,' he explained as he showed Tess the jar then rubbed a small amount between his hands to warm it up before spreading it on her skin. 'We have it on hand for guests who swim and snorkel over the reef, fascinated by the colours, then when they get stiff and sore later on they realise they've done too much.'

'I had no idea of the many uses of coconuts before I came here,' Tess told him. Her voice sounded calm and self-possessed so it was obvious she wasn't having the same trouble he was with the situation.

Determined to hide any emotion, he smoothed the cream onto the skin in the small of her back, checking he had the right place before beginning to massage it in, gently gliding his hands over her skin, up the spine and down again, out towards where her skin stretched over the new baby, and down to the small indentation right at the base of her spine.

And as hard as it was to be stroking her soft-as-satin skin, even harder was getting his head around the scarlet bikini panties peeking from above the shorts she'd lowered just a little—panties that matched the scarlet strap of the bra across the middle of her back.

Who'd have thought there was sexy underwear hidden beneath the prim blue shirts she always wore?

And why?

He rubbed his hands up and down again, kneading along her spine, finding parts he knew were sore when she flinched.

He'd always been of the opinion women wore sexy underwear for their menfolk.

Was there a man lurking somewhere in her life?

Someone she'd met after her decision to have the baby?

Was that why she'd fled to Tihoroa? Not to get away from family pressures but to work out how to tell her family and the baby's family that she'd met another man?

Although wouldn't they be pleased for her?

Unless the new man didn't want another man's child?

Yes, that could pose a problem.

Questions with no answers, but the really big question was why he was even thinking about this.

Because of her sexy red underwear?

What was the matter with him?

'Oh, that is bliss! Thank you, Eduardo,' she whispered, and his libido fired up again, thinking of the whisper in other contexts. Now he knew what the matter was with him—unrequited lust!

He should be ashamed of himself. Concentrate on the massage! But as his hands moved to the side he felt the flutter.

'The baby kicked me,' he said, startled to have felt it, and equally startled by the delight he felt, keeping his hand against the swell to feel the movement again.

'She must have felt you'd strayed into her territory,' Tess said, a teasing lilt in her voice.

'She? Her?' Eduardo queried. 'You know it's a girl?'

'Rose tells me it is,' she said, and turned her head to look at him. 'I'd been happy to think it might be either, but now—well, a little girl would be such fun, not that a boy wouldn't be fun, but a little girl. We could be friends...'

Her grey-green eyes looked clouded, smoky—as if...

But if she'd been as affected by the massage as he was, surely she couldn't be carrying on such a normal conversation about the sex of her unborn child.

And remember that child, del Riga, he warned himself. This is not a woman you can enjoy for a short time then leave with no prods of conscience. This is a woman with a baby to consider.

She'd turned away, her head once again resting on her arms, and he dug his thumbs into the spaces between her ribs, following the line of her spine right up to where the scarlet slashed across her pale skin.

'Undo it and keep going,' she begged. 'That is just too good for you to stop there.'

But undoing it proved his undoing, for her breasts swung free, heavy with pregnancy—blue-veined milky whiteness.

'This is impossible,' he croaked, although his thumbs kept going right up to her neck where he massaged the soft indentations beneath her skull, bringing more whimpers of delight. 'I'm only human, Tess, and I haven't been with a woman for a long time.'

He felt the shudder that rippled through her.

'Or me with a man, but is that all it is, Eduardo? And if so, does it make it wrong?'

She eased out from under his ministering fingers, grabbed her shirt and held it in front of her as she turned to face him.

Smoky-eyed!

Pleading with him, but silently.

Wanting him to make the decision.

He took the hand that wasn't clutching the shirt to her breasts and eased her to her feet so they were facing each other, then he leaned forward and kissed her gently on the lips.

Too gently, for she sought more, her mouth fastening on his, feasting—or was it he who feasted?

All he knew for sure was that his blood was pounding through his veins, his body on fire, heat zeroing down to his groin.

All this from a kiss?

Stand back.

Think about it.

Don't push now.

The warning words from his brain got through eventually to his body and he did stand back, though he kept a hand on her shoulder in case her legs were feeling as unreliable as his.

'I'm sorry—that shouldn't have happened. I'm putting it down to pregnancy hormones,' she said, but her eyes told him she was having trouble believing it.

'I'm not pregnant,' he pointed out, and Tess half smiled, then shook her head. She wanted this man as she'd never wanted anyone. She knew it was just physical, and maybe pregnancy related, but the ache of need seemed to blot out all other considerations while the limitations of her time on Tihoroa provided a kind of safety net.

It would be like a holiday romance—a memory to take out now and then, polish up until it shone again, and sigh over.

Could she do it?

Dared she?

'Because it would only be a temporary thing...' she began, her voice faint and shaking with the temerity of what she was almost suggesting, hoping Eduardo would pick up her thoughts so she didn't have to say it.

He studied her for a moment then rubbed his knuckles gently down her cheek.

'I have nothing to offer you, Tess. Like the pirate you first thought me, I'd take you then send you on your way,' Eduardo said.

'But don't you see? That's just why it could work.' Was this super-cautious Tess Beresford uttering these words? 'No ties for either of us—time limited...'

He shook his head.

'You might think that is enough, but for how long? How soon would you begin to feel uneasy with yourself? How soon would you regret such a rash decision? Unless, of course, affairs are a commonplace undertaking for you. Is that it? Is that why you are still unmarried? Do you indulge in passion with men you don't care for so you can remain true in your heart to your Grant? And I thought *I* was an emotional desert!'

His voice had deepened as his anger took hold, but his accusations made Tess equally angry.

'How dare you suggest that? I have *never* had an affair!' she snapped, clutching her shirt even more tightly to her chest. 'And why I ever thought I might start on such a path with a man like you is beyond my comprehension. Now, thank you for the back rub and goodnight, Dr del Riga.'

Eduardo left, but as he walked back to the jetty where he'd left his boat, he thought he knew the answer to her question. They were two emotionally isolated human beings, coming together by chance, finding a mutual attraction, but deep down probably seeking something else.

Seeking love?

He shuddered, shook off the thought and kept walking.

CHAPTER FOUR

TESS WAS SURE she wouldn't sleep, so unsettling had the massage and kiss been, not to mention the harsh words that had followed, but when she woke up to another bright, sunny, Tihoroan morning, she couldn't remember lying awake at all.

And she certainly hadn't agonised over Eduardo, or even felt more than a mite embarrassed that she'd virtually proposed an affair to him, and he'd turned her down.

Maybe pregnancy had turned her brain to mush, so anything at all worrying or controversial—or maybe anything not needing immediate brain attention—simply sank beneath the sludge without trace.

Although meeting up with him later would be the test. After all, they hadn't parted on the best of terms.

How to tackle it?

That was easy—pretend it hadn't happened. Think about the baby—baby names for a little girl—think about Grant, or schooldays or anything to take your mind off the effect Eduardo del Riga has on you! And above all, pretend last night never happened.

Having delivered this short lecture to herself, she got out of bed.

Aware a big day lay ahead of her, she didn't swim in the lagoon, a practice she'd continued in spite of Eduardo warning her off. It was close, and more than that, she didn't feel comfortable revealing her pregnant body down at the beach where the others swam.

But this morning she simply showered, dressed and headed straight for the canteen. At six in the morning, there were few people eating, which made it even easier to pick out Eduardo, sharing a table with Albert, pointing at Albert's breakfast, no doubt lecturing *him* on the dangers of cholesterol.

Tess felt a flutter in her heart and rested her hand on her belly, telling herself it was her daughter kicking. Daughter? Could she really be believing Rose's diagnosis? Was the tropical heat getting to her? What was the expression? Going troppo?

Surely not!

Although that might explain last night's little episode…

Selecting fruit and yoghurt, juice and some toast, Tess carried her tray to the table, eager to know what lay ahead—less eager to be close to Eduardo. Amy was a nice name for a little girl, or Amelia, Annabelle, Alicia…

Was she wearing scarlet underwear? was Eduardo's first thought, followed closely by, Why did she look so rested when he had tossed and turned all night, frustration and regret fighting within him, tension from the angry words tightening his nerves?

OK, so the limited time she had on the island meant they probably could have enjoyed a brief affair, but he'd never been an affair sort of man, marrying Ilse when they'd both been young—probably in retrospect far too young—and expecting to stay married to her for ever. Wife, family, work—that was the way it had always been for del Rigas. Which was why, attractive as Caroline had been, he'd refused first to believe she had been coming on to him, then, when she'd asked outright if he was interested in a little extra-marital sex, he'd said no.

Probably far too clearly, and possibly rudely if her extreme reaction to his refusal was any indication.

But why had he said no to Tess? Worse, why had he accused her of—what? Being like Caroline who moved from man to man without a second thought? Yep, that's more or less what he'd said.

No wonder Tess had reacted angrily. Now here she was, walking straight towards them.

Smiling!

Calm as the lagoon on a windless night.

'Good morning!' she said brightly and Eduardo realised she was far better at pretence than he was.

Or maybe she didn't feel what he felt. Didn't feel the earth tilt dangerously on its axis whenever they were together. Didn't feel the heat, and the charge in the atmosphere.

Didn't feel guilt over the argument the previous evening…

Oh, she'd admitted to attraction, but it must be a feeble thing compared to his, that she could act so—so together!

'Good morning,' he replied, carefully polite, determined not to reveal his uncertainty.

Or the heat and tilting axis…

'You get seasick?' Albert asked, and Eduardo watched her face still, then her brows draw together uncertainly.

'I don't know. Apart from ferries on the river or Sydney Harbour I've never been out in a boat.'

'He's teasing you,' Eduardo assured her, not liking to see

that little frown. 'The waters between the islands are calm ninety per cent of the time. It's only if there's a cyclone around we get rough weather. The ocean swells break against the fringing reefs that surround the entire island group, which means the waters within them are protected.'

'But you should eat ginger anyway, in case the motion of the boat upsets you.'

Albert lifted a piece of glacé ginger from a plate in the middle of the table and sliced it thinly, dropping the slices into Tess's yoghurt.

'Thanks,' she said, and meant it. 'I ate ginger early in my pregnancy—it does help with nausea. Do you grow it here?'

'Everyone grows it,' Albert told her. 'You will often smell the scent of ginger flowers as you walk around the island. Eduardo has it growing beneath his deck so he smells it as he sits and looks out to sea.'

Eduardo had been happy to let Albert take over the conversation, but this bit of it prompted an image of himself and Tess, sitting on his wide deck, watching the sunset and smelling the ginger flowers.

He glanced at her and, seeing her concentration on her breakfast, watched her for a while, not thinking of her underwear this time but wondering about inviting her for dinner that evening.

Although she'd be tired after the clinic run—being out on the boat was always tiring, in a very healthy way. He could ask her to dinner tomorrow night…

Having her in his home? What *was* he thinking?

They'd settled there'd be no affair, but to invite opportunity? He must be crazy. At least she had excuses for craziness. She was pregnant. She was vulnerable.

And she already had enough complications in her life…

'So which island do we visit first?' she asked, looking to Albert for a reply.

Albert pulled a clean serviette from the holder in the middle of the table and began to sketch their route, marking in the islands they would pass and pointing out which ones they would visit.

'Only three stops but it takes all day?' Tess asked, as she studied the fragile paper map, tracing the line they'd take with one finger.

'More than all day if we don't keep things moving,' Eduardo told her, and Tess, who'd done her best to ignore his presence since her first greeting to him, finally had to look his way.

The sad thing was, the argument notwithstanding, Eduardo still looked as good to her this morning as he had since the first moment they'd met. And her body responded accordingly. Which was probably why she'd said what she had last night, shocking the socks off Eduardo—not that he wore socks—by virtually suggesting they indulge in an affair.

And while he may have been shocked, she'd been even more shocked. All her life—her adult, post-Grant life—she'd thought things through, made little lists of pros and cons. This was different. She'd stepped into another world and once there had discovered physical responses she'd never thought she'd experience again. So why not, she'd thought last night, for four short weeks, indulge themselves and not think about the consequences? Though why any man could be attracted to a woman as pregnant as she was she didn't quite understand…

'Ready?'

Albert's question reminded her of the day that lay ahead, and she finished the last piece of pawpaw on her plate, scooped the final spoonful of yoghurt and ginger into her mouth, and nodded.

'More than ready,' she said, pushing her chair back with her calves as she stood up, then catching the heel of her sandal in one of the chair legs. Eduardo was quick, reaching out to steady her—his touch anything but steadying as far as her nerves were concerned.

'Thanks,' she managed, moving so he was no longer in touching distance, hurriedly following Albert out of the canteen and down towards the jetty where a sizeable boat with twin outboards bobbed gently on the water, a small orange dinghy bobbing behind it.

Philippe was waiting there, a backpack slung across his shoulders.

'She's twenty foot, twin-hulled for stability and runs with two eighty horsepower—' Albert began.

'I think a woman whose only previous boating experience has been river and harbour ferries might get confused with engine power.' Eduardo broke in to Albert's proud description of the boat and held out his hand to help Tess down into the craft, again steadying her until she took a seat up front, next to the steering-wheel.

Did you call them steering-wheels in boats?

In front of them was a small cabin, with bunks on either side, equipment stacked on every available surface. Tess could see a collapsible stretcher, a battery-operated monitor, oxygen bottles strapped into place against the wall. Or was it the hull?

'The stretcher, should we need to transport a bedridden patient, slots in across the bunks with special straps to hold it steady.'

Philippe had taken a seat right at the stern of the boat

and looked ready to fall asleep. Eduardo was sitting behind her, back to back, but had turned sideways in his seat so he could point out the equipment.

His shoulder brushed against hers and she could feel the warmth of his body, so it was difficult to focus on his words. Then Albert appeared and took his seat, starting up the engines and giving orders to Philippe about mooring ropes.

The engines roared then quietened and the boat slid away from the jetty so smoothly it was only the sight of the island receding that convinced Tess they were moving.

The trip was unbelievable, the sea changing colour according to its depth and to whether or not they were passing over coral. So sometimes it was azure blue, then aquamarine, or palest green, then dark purple.

'It's beautiful,' she breathed, leaning out the window beside her for a better view, then looking forward again so she wouldn't miss anything ahead of them. The sound of the motors changed and their speed lessened. Albert swung the wheel to the right, and there, missed by Tess as she'd watched the changing colours of the water, was another island.

'Kiki,' Albert said, and as there were no people in sight Tess assumed he was telling her the name of the island. The boat slid quietly through a lagoon not unlike the one Tess swam in, then swung round and in front of them was the settlement—a number of thatched huts set around a larger hut, like chicks gathered around a mother hen.

'No jetty?' she queried as Albert nosed the boat up onto the beach.

'Shoes-off time,' Albert said as Philippe slid off the side of the boat and pulled the anchor up the beach, making it fast in the sand. He returned to hold the boat steady, Eduardo disembarking next into the knee-deep water. But when it was Tess's turn to get over the side of the boat into the shallow water, Eduardo forestalled her, lifting her easily into his arms and carrying her up the beach.

She considered a token protest—she weighed too much—but it felt so good to be…cared for? Then, as he set her on her feet on the dry sand, she laughed to herself. It had been a gesture of politeness, nothing more. Doubtless he'd have lifted Janne or Mathilde the same way.

But the strength of his arms, the ease with which he'd carried her, had stirred something deeper than desire. Had Rose been right? Did a woman need a man's arms around her from time to time to make her complete?

This was no time to be thinking of men's arms or completion. A small group of islanders was coming towards them, wide smiles of greeting splitting their faces.

'You are welcome,' the first woman said, taking Tess's hand then resting her free hand on Tess's belly. 'You and your daughter.'

Tess laughed, aloud this time, and, forgetting the awkwardness of the previous night, turned to Eduardo.

'Do they all have second sight?' she asked.

Eduardo heard the question but couldn't reply, his mind frozen by the sight of Tess laughing, her long hair tousled by the wind, her eyes gleaming with delight, looking up at him as if asking him to share the joke—to share her joy in this wonderful new experience she was having.

His mind frozen by the thought it might be more than attraction he felt towards her…

Love at first sight?

Impossible!

Yet as she turned back to speak to the people welcoming her, he had to wonder because he wanted her, and not, he suspected, just physically. He wanted to see that smile in her eyes and hear her laughter all the time—wanted her as part of his life.

Which was also impossible, for what had he, of all people, to offer such a woman?

Any woman?

Not trust, that was for sure.

Not even an untainted name.

Tess followed the laughing, chatting group up to the largest of the huts, which appeared to be a communal meeting hall. People were ranged around the walls, while others, mostly in family groups, sat on mats on the floor.

'Do we see them all?' she asked the woman who was guiding her. 'Are they all ill?'

'No, no!' The woman laughed at the idea all the people in the hall might be sick. 'They come for the socialising. Some of the children might need shots, or the old people new medicine, but others come to talk to Eduardo about things, and Albert's relatives come to talk to him about the new baby. Others just come. It is a nice day out, clinic day.'

'It certainly has that picnic atmosphere,' Tess agreed, though she was wondering just where she might be immunising children or seeing elderly patients.

'Through here.'

She turned but this time it was Albert who read her mind, waving her towards a woven screen. Once behind it, she saw an almost normal clinic set-up—an examination table, chairs and a trolley. Albert set down the box he'd carried from the boat, then Philippe appeared with a small cool box filled with drugs. The box held the files and beneath them gloves, swabs, boxes of syringes and needles, disinfectant and various dressings, everything she'd need—even a small sharps container for used needles.

Setting up the trolley took only a few minutes, so she was ready when Eduardo appeared.

'Fast learner,' he said, but the smile he offered with the words appeared strained.

Considering how they'd parted last night, this wasn't surprising, but she was making a good job of pretence so why couldn't he?

Unless his anger and hurtful reply to her suggestion had been his way of saying he had no interest in her and he was now deeply embarrassed, knowing how she felt.

Could that be it?

She shook her head, sure the attraction she felt wasn't all one-sided. Well, almost sure…

He was checking the trolley, then the contents of the cool box, so she was able to study him, but when, apparently satisfied, he turned back towards her, she pretended to be fascinated by the file of Millie Sanrawana, who had ongoing problems with bladder infections.

'All set?' he asked, and she nodded, then listened as he explained that they would see whoever needed to be seen before joining the islanders at morning tea.

'You eat a lot on clinic days,' he said, a wry smile curling his lips.

The sight of it—that kindly, teasing smile—sent Tess's heart into conniptions.

He's just a man, she reminded herself, but that seemed to make things worse. Pretence might work on the surface, but it was failing miserably inside.

Yet they worked together well, Tess finding she could anticipate what he wanted nearly as easily as the island people read her mind. Within an hour the clinic was finished, seven patients seen and no major calamities or fearful diagnoses.

'Now we eat,' Eduardo announced, touching Tess lightly on the back to guide her back around the screen.

The touch was impersonal—almost too impersonal—and once again she had the impression of a shift in the delicate balance between the two of them—a shift away from the passion that had briefly flared the previous evening.

'I'll pack the boxes first. You'll have people you have to see so I'll join you later.'

He turned towards her, frowning slightly, perhaps at the carefully casual tone in which she'd uttered the words.

'Tess?'

What was he asking? She tried to read his face, but apart from a slight puzzlement there was nothing there to read.

'Go!' she said, and pointed to where the screen split to allow passage.

He went, and she breathed a sigh of relief.

She repacked the boxes, checked the cool box, then followed him into the hall to ask someone for some ice to replace the rapidly warming freezer block in the box.

'Ah, we give you a new frozen block and keep the old one,' the woman who'd first greeted her explained. 'And at the next island the same thing. We are well organised, no?'

'You are indeed,' Tess assured her, then felt a tremor along her nerves and guessed Eduardo was approaching.

'I've brought you juice and some yam cookies—you'll find them different but tasty.'

He set a tray down on a chair near where Tess was standing.

'You're ready to leave?' she guessed, and he nodded.

'Just about. Albert will take the big box down to the boat and when you're ready...'

She drank the juice then tucked the cookies in her pocket.

'I'll eat them on the boat,' she explained, taking the replacement freezer block from her new friend and ducking back behind the screen to pack it into the cool box.

Two more islands, two more clinics, and everywhere the same friendly, welcoming smiles and happy faces.

'These people must be sad sometimes!' she protested when they boarded the boat for the trip home.

'Of course,' Eduardo agreed. 'Like people all over the world, they grieve when a loved one is ill, or dies. They worry if a pearling boat is late returning to the jetty, but generally they lead uncomplicated lives, content with their island paradise. A lot of the anguish in the Western world is caused by discontent—by people not being content with what they have but always wanting more.'

Tess thought about it, nodding her agreement, then nodding sleepily as the day in the sun and on the sea caught up with her.

'I'll clear a bunk so you can lie down and sleep,' Eduardo said. Worried she'd fall off her seat if she fell asleep where she sat, she didn't argue. So she was sound asleep when the alarm came through and the boat changed direction, heading not back to the main island but out to sea, pitching across the swell, Albert pushing the engines as fast as he dared.

Voices woke her, voices shouting—Albert's voice and Eduardo's and panicky voices yelling in some foreign language. Was it Tihoroan? Most of the islanders spoke English but amongst themselves used a kind of musical pidgin. This sounded different. And the boat was pitching, tipping sideways, causing more yelling from Albert.

Tess struggled to her feet and cautiously came out of the cabin.

'You sit!' Eduardo ordered, and she was so surprised by the force of the order she sat.

And looked around…

A surreal sight greeted her bewildered gaze. Half a timber boat bobbed in front of them, only the upper structure of what she assumed was a wheelhouse still above the water. And clinging to it were what seemed like dozens of people, all wailing and crying out, while more swam or dog-paddled towards the Tihoroan boat, some holding onto pieces of timber to stay afloat or holding children on inadequate bits of debris.

'I can swim well, I can help,' Tess said when she realised the magnitude of the disaster being played out in front of her.

'You sit,' Eduardo repeated. 'I need to organise them somehow, get the children aboard first, then their mothers. We have lifebuoys we can throw to others and we have the dinghy. Alberto is taking that to collect children still on the sinking boat. Once on board, they're all yours. Stack them on the bunks, wrapped together to stay warm, but until then it's best not to move around as people will try to climb aboard and we don't want to tip over.'

Tess remained seated, seeing the sense in what he was saying, listening to him speak to the people in the water, first in English, then in French and finally in another language she didn't understand—Portuguese?

'OK, first load,' he said, and Tess saw the little dinghy coming closer, crammed with small, dark-haired children, some screaming, others eerily silent. Eduardo leaned forward and lifted each child out, passing him or her to Tess who gave each one a quick hug before carrying them into the cabin. Soon she had nine children, some little more than babies, lined up on one of the bunks. She found water bottles and passed them to the bigger ones, indicating to them to drink and pass the bottle on. Then she wrapped them in what blankets she could find, huddling them together into one group of four and one of five.

And all the while large dark eyes watched her every move, fear in most of the faces, uncertainty in the others.

'It's OK,' she kept on saying, chafing the small cold feet, tipping water into unresponsive lips, finally picking up the smallest of the children, a little girl, and cuddling her. She felt the boat move as more people came on board, then three women tried to cram through the cabin door at once and stuck there, shrieking at each other, so the children began to cry.

Tess sorted out the tangle, but as she was about to let them through in a more orderly fashion to reclaim their child or children, Eduardo stopped her.

'One by one,' he said. 'Let them take a child or children then come back up here and sit on the deck. If they all go in at once, we'll be bow-heavy and could sink.'

Tess wasn't sure the women understood so she kept the little one in her arms and took up a position near the door, letting one woman in, then indicating she could take her child outside, until one by one her charges disappeared.

Except for the silent, quiescent infant in her arms. No one had claimed her, and fear gripped Tess's heart. Had the mother drowned? They had to be refugees, these people, fleeing from their homeland, paying money to unscrupulous dealers in human misery who put them on unsafe vessels and sent them out to sea.

How many perished that no one ever knew about?

She hugged the little girl more tightly.

'Is a bunk clear?' Eduardo asked, and Tess's attention turned back to the present situation. 'We've an injured man.'

She watched Eduardo bend and lift a slight young man into his arms, carrying him into the cabin and setting him down on a bunk.

'I need to go back—we can't let them tip us over. Can you check him out? ABC, you know the drill.'

Tess nodded, then sat the little girl at the foot of the bunk, where she grabbed hold of the young man's foot as if needing human contact.

Or maybe needing someone she knew?

Her father?

Surely the sick man was little more than a teenager.

Questions were still rattling through Tess's head as she began her examination, checking his airway was clear, listening to his breathing, pulling a stethoscope from the clinic box to listen to his chest, hearing a wheeze that could be water in his lungs or an infection—possibly pneumonia.

Possibly bird flu?

Shock held her motionless for an instant.

There had been so much publicity about the likelihood of a pandemic she couldn't help but feel queasy, just thinking about it.

She lifted his wrist and felt the heat in his skin. Was he running a temperature or suffering an overdose of the sun? She doubted it was sunburn, although sunstroke could lead to fever. Could it lead to unconsciousness? She didn't know, but sunstroke was definitely a more comforting option than bird flu.

His pulse was weak but regular—but, then, he'd probably been a very healthy young man before whatever had happened to him recently.

She turned him on his side in the recovery position and began a physical examination, feeling all over his skull for signs of an injury that might explain his unconscious state. No lumps or bumps, no pieces of bone moving under her fingers, and his eyes, when she prised open his eyelids and shone a small torch into them, responded equally to light.

Dehydration? She pinched the skin on the back of his hand and found it remained in a pinched position. But dehydration wouldn't send an otherwise healthy young man into a coma.

Alfred had said the boat was equipped with most of the gear an ambulance carried so there should be fluid packs somewhere. Not in the box they'd taken ashore for clinics, but maybe in another box. She searched through the equipment on the other bunk, finding nothing, then realised both bunks had storage space beneath them. She'd just found a bag of saline and the tubing and cannula she'd need to attach it to the young man when Eduardo appeared.

'We've taken all we can take on board, and have more in the dinghy. Albert sent out a radio alert as soon as we saw the sinking vessel, and one of the pearling fleet's boats is in sight to pick up the rest of the survivors. We've left lifebuoys for those still in the water and we're going to sail very slowly towards home. The pearling boat will probably catch up with us and take on board the people we have in the dinghy. Are you OK?'

Tess nodded, then indicated her patient.

'I can't find any obvious injury but he's febrile so it could be an infection. I was just going to start some fluid running into him.'

'You're confident about finding a vein?'

Tess nodded. In hospitals doctors were usually called in to insert cannulas for drips, but most nurses could do it equally efficiently.

'Good,' he said. 'I've a couple of badly cut people out there and one suspected broken leg. I want to make them as comfortable as possible as it will be a long trip home.'

Home? Where was home for these people? Tess wondered. Not the place they'd left—not any more…

The little girl had lain down, one hand still clamped on the young man's leg. Tess tucked a blanket around her, then swabbed the back of the young man's hand where a network of veins offered her a choice of sites for the cannula.

Once satisfied with the placement, she taped it into place and joined the drip tubing. The closure on the small porthole in the cabin served to hang the bag of fluid and within minutes of beginning the exercise she had it flowing into the young man's vein.

She checked his pulse again, and listened to the rattly sounds in his chest, felt the heat in his skin, which had already dried out his wet clothing. Needing something to do, she began to bathe him to cool his body, praying the young man's illness would be something innocuous, and all the while the boat moved steadily towards the main island.

Let it not be bird flu…

At one stage she poked her head out of the cabin, calling to ask Eduardo if he needed help.

'Everything under control here,' he called back, although she could hear stress in his voice and wondered if this situation could ever be considered 'under control.'

The thrum of heavy engines told her the pearling boat was drawing near, and she felt the change in the boat's movement as Albert throttled back then held the motors in neutral as the bigger boat came alongside.

Excited shouts sounded from both sets of passengers, then orders were yelled as the people from the little dinghy were transferred to the larger vessel.

'Take us home, Albert,' Eduardo said when the transfer was complete and the big boat had moved away.

Albert must have been waiting for the word, for he revved the engines and the bow of the clinic boat lifted out of the water as the vessel forged ahead for Tihoroa.

'Do you know where they've come from?' Tess asked when Eduardo appeared in the doorway of the cabin, bracing himself against the jamb as the boat sped homewards.

'Some Asian country, maybe the Middle East or even Afghanistan,' he replied, his voice heavy with concern and maybe a little despair. 'I think they may be afraid to tell us.'

Tess nodded. 'Will you send them on to Australia?' she asked, thinking of quarantine and health testing.

'I doubt they'll take them,' Eduardo replied. 'Boat people who get into Australian waters are taken to one of the Pacific islands and processed there, but these people are in our waters—Tihoroan waters. The Tihoroan governing council will have to make a decision about their future.'

'And their health?' Tess asked, nodding towards the very sick young man on the bunk.

'Our problem for a while—yours and mine. You're thinking bird flu?'

She had to smile that their thoughts had matched again, but then she shook her head.

'No way,' she said, denying her deepest fears. 'I'm thinking very positively that it's pneumonia—even double or triple pneumonia. Quadruple pneumonia?'

Eduardo smiled back at her, a weak effort but still a smile, then he reached out and brushed his hand across her hair.

'I hope you're right,' he murmured, his eyes going from the patient to Tess then back to the patient. Finally, he gave an impatient sigh. 'What a fool I was asking you to care for him. You could have looked after the cuts and bruises and the broken leg—and not come into contact with him at all.'

'If all these people have been cooped up on a boat together, then any number of them could be affected by whatever ails him, so having me do other things would have made no difference. But now I have nursed him, I'll stay with him. Others should be masked and gloved if they have to come close, at least until we find out what is wrong.'

She paused, then caught his eyes.

'And that includes you,' she said, her stern voice daring him to argue.

Which he did.

'It's not right, you nursing him,' he protested. 'What about your child?'

Tess had her own fears about that, but no way would she reveal them to Eduardo.

'I've had every kind of flu injection ever invented. Apparently flu viruses mutate so swiftly that often the two or three strains identified at the start of each year as likely to be bad—the ones they develop the vaccine specifically for—have changed by the time the flu season starts, but research has found the vaccines can prevent many strains of flu, not just the ones for which it was invented.'

'You know so much about flu vaccines?'

He sounded intrigued and though she could have felt aggrieved by the implications of his question, she didn't.

'I love reading scientific magazines and articles,' she

admitted. 'In fact, I was hoping, while I was here, to find out more about your work with stem cells.'

Mental headshake. She needed to be seeing less of Eduardo, not more. Although maybe he was protective of his research and would ignore her comment.

'I'd be happy to show you my lab and explain the work to you.'

Damn! Now she'd really made things difficult for herself.

'But right now,' he continued, his voice stern, 'my concern is for you and your child.'

He nodded towards her swollen belly, but she refused to admit her own uneasiness. He was already worried for her, as he worried for everyone—so no way would she lump her worries onto him as well.

She gave a casual shrug.

'Nurses are vaccinated and inoculated against just about everything known to man,' she assured him. 'And very few infections cross the placenta at this late stage, so the child will be all right.'

She wasn't one hundred percent certain about that last bit but guessed Eduardo wouldn't know any more than she did, so she met his eyes, challenging him to argue.

But Eduardo's thoughts were on another track.

'Even if its mother dies?' he snapped, infuriated by the situation—knowing she was right in theory but desperately concerned for her.

She looked at him for a moment, then turned to put her hand on the little girl curled up at the foot of the bed.

'Should my child be any more special than this child?' she said quietly. 'Should she be guaranteed a mother when this child hasn't got one?'

Her voice broke as she spoke and Eduardo wanted nothing more than to go to her and put his arms around her, to hold her against his body and assure her everything would be all right. But, as if sensing his intention, she held up her hand.

'Masked and gowned and gloved,' she reminded him.

CHAPTER FIVE

THE ISLANDERS WERE devastated when Eduardo decreed they could not take the traumatised people into their homes. Naturally warm-hearted and welcoming, they found it hard to understand Eduardo's edict that they have no contact with the strangers.

'It's for your own safety,' he told them at a gathering in the meeting hall that Tess didn't attend, as she, too, had been quarantined, having insisted she nurse the young man in the spare bed in her hut. 'Remember back in history when the sailors brought new diseases to the islands and many people died. This could happen now, so we'll use all six of the visitors' huts for the people to live in while we find out what is wrong with the young man and test the others to make sure they are healthy.'

Tess heard about it all from Janne, who brought an evening meal across for Tess and the little girl, leaving it on the front step of the hut and standing some six feet away from Tess as they spoke.

'Eduardo looked up bird flu on the internet and said it is not easy to catch from one human to another. He said to stay three to six feet away and has drawn a line in the sand around the visitor huts for us to stay behind.'

A line in the sand, Tess thought. Is that what had happened to these people? At some stage had they, too, drawn a metaphorical line in the sand and said, no more, packing up a few possessions and paying money to escape?

Janne explained that Eduardo was taking blood from all the newcomers to send on the mail plane in the morning, and that he would be coming to Tess's hut last.

Tess looked across to where the other visitors' huts were, sheltered under palm trees, separated by bright flowering shrubs and bushes. The people from the boat were safe now, but how did they feel, shut away like they were?

Maybe they were too exhausted to care.

She took the tray inside, and saw the little girl stirring on the bed.

'We're going to have dinner,' she said to her, setting the tray down on the small desk, before going to wash her hands then lift the child, wash her hands and set her on the chair at the desk.

Tess drew one of the comfortable lounge chairs close to the desk and began to feed the little girl.

'Fish,' she said, pointing to the delicate white flesh before offering a teaspoonful to the child.

Like a baby bird opening its beak to its mother, the little girl's mouth opened and Tess slid the morsel inside.

They had finished the fish, mashed potatoes and peas and were starting on the dessert of fruit and custard when Tess realised she was opening her mouth in unison with the child.

She laughed to herself, wondering if this was something all mothers did—if she'd do it as she spoon-fed her own baby.

When they were down to the last few spoonfuls of custard, she handed the little girl the spoon. Dark eyes studied it, moving it around in her hand until she found a comfortable position, then she dug into the custard and finished the rest herself.

Tess clapped her hands and told her she was clever and a shy smile spread across the little face. Unable to resist, Tess took her in her arms and hugged her tightly, pressing kisses on the salt-crusted hair.

'I'm going to eat my dinner then we'll both have a shower,' she told her new friend. The little girl seemed to understand, snuggling down beside Tess in the big chair—as close as she could get to sitting on Tess's lap, considering a lap was something missing from Tess's configuration at the moment.

'You need some toys—something to play with,' she told her, then remembered Rose's gift of shells.

Certain neither Rose or her own baby would mind this child playing with the shells, she got up and found the little basket, and set it on the floor. She put the child down beside it, picking out two shells that matched and putting them side by side.

The little girl understood the game and soon had lines of shells along the painted floorboards.

Tess finished her meal, stacked the dishes on the tray and walked to the door, intending to return it to the front step then come back inside. But large, bulky packages drew her attention. They were the requisite six feet away, stacked as if Eduardo's line in the sand held them back.

'Is someone there?' Tess called, wondering when the parcels had appeared, but no one answered so she walked towards them then smiled when she realised what she was seeing. Woven baskets and cardboard boxes full of toys and clothes. Clothes to fit a very small girl—clothes to fit a slight young man. There was fruit as well, bananas and split coconuts and luscious mangoes.

Tess looked around again, wanting to thank someone—anyone—for all this bounty, but the area was deserted, although she could see similar dark piles in front of the other huts.

The islanders may not have been able to take these people into their homes so they were showing their hospitality and warmth and love in another way—with their generosity.

Carrying things into her hut, Tess couldn't help but be grateful she'd had the opportunity to come to this magical place. She may be in a muddle over Eduardo, but that was a minor complication compared to what she was learning from the islanders.

Be content with what you have and show generosity of spirit—these two things would remain as influences in her life for a long time.

She stacked all the goodies inside the door, the little girl coming over to have a look, seeing a rather tatty-looking doll and putting her hand tentatively towards it.

Tess lifted it out of the basket and gave it to her, then was surprised to see the little girl return to the shells and stack them all neatly back into the basket before turning her attention to the doll, examining its clothes before rocking it in her arms as one would a baby.

Had she had a baby brother or sister?

Or just a doll, some time in her life?

Useless conjecture! Tess dug through the treasure trove—pirates again—until she found a small pink nightdress.

She checked her patient—no change—washed her hands then led her small friend into the bathroom, stripping off the ragged dress and knickers then turning on the shower, stripping herself as well so they could shower together. Without a bath this seemed the best way to accustom the child to the shower.

Then, clean and dressed, the little girl in the nightdress and Tess in a casual shift in case Eduardo did come later, they went back into the main room, where the little girl picked up her doll and headed for the young man's bed.

'You sleep here with me,' Tess said to her, putting her back in the big bed where she'd slept earlier while they had been settling the young man into his bed.

She seemed to understand for she turned on her side and snuggled down, talking now to the doll in some language Tess didn't understand.

He had to see the youth and take some blood, but walking into Tess's hut after what had occurred the previous night slowed Eduardo's feet as he made his way towards it.

Although last night was surely forgotten, swept away by all that had occurred since and by the problem of the new-comers to the island.

Not entirely swept away, he realised when Tess came to the door in answer to his quiet call. She was dressed in a long cotton shift in swirly colours of blue and green, her hair flowing around her shoulders, so she looked for all the world like a mermaid or some other magical creature.

His heart thudded, his groin ached, and his temper rose.

Not this time because of his reactions but because she was here, and was in potential danger and, whichever way he looked at it, he was partly responsible.

'This was the stupidest idea I've ever heard, you taking the young man into your hut,' he muttered at her, fiddling with the mask he'd ordered all the medical staff to wear when near any of the boat people.

'And good evening to you too,' the mermaid said, stepping out onto the small deck in front of her hut so they could speak without disturbing those inside.

Even more infuriating was the fact that he couldn't control his response.

'It's not a joking matter, Tess!' he growled, knowing at least part of his anger was at himself—not only for involving her, but also for his physical reaction to her presence.

'Of course it's not,' she snapped right back at him. 'The man is sick, very sick, and it's our duty to take care of him, not to argue over who does what. You know it makes sense for me to nurse him, and even more sense to nurse him here rather than in the clinic, where there would be a risk of spreading infection to the islanders.'

He sighed but refused to admit, in words, that she was right. He changed the subject instead.

'I've been reading up on bird flu—the risk of it spreading from human to human is very slight. In fact, there's only one known case—or set of cases—and that's a family in Indonesia where eight people contracted it from one infected child.'

'If that's the case,' Tess said, puzzled by the information, 'why has there been a worldwide panic over a possible pandemic?'

Eduardo's smile lit up his eyes.

'You answered that yourself the other day. Flu viruses mutate so swiftly it's only a matter of time until some variation of it becomes transmissible through human populations. But so far in most of the cases, those infected have actually been in direct contact with sick birds.'

'Do we know if this is possible—that the young man could have had contact with birds? Have you been able to talk to any of them?'

She moved closer and he smelt the scent she used—or was it just the scent of Tess? Citrusy—kind of green, like her dress, although he wasn't sure perfume came in green.

'A number of the men and one of the women speak English, but most didn't know each other before they gathered to get the boat. Apparently some are from refugee camps, using money sent from family abroad to escape, while others have fled directly from their countries of origin, hearing about underground escape routes and following them. The woman said your young man came from a village not far from hers and one day he returned home to find his entire family slaughtered—well, almost his entire family. The little girl is his sister. She was hidden in a feed bin out the back of the house.'

Even now, repeating it for the second time, for he'd told the village elders, Eduardo found the words difficult to say, having to speak through a lump in his throat as he put himself in the young man's place—coming home to such horror and devastation.

He watched Tess brush her hand impatiently across her eyes and swallow hard, and knew she was picturing it as well. He wanted to go to her, to hug her, but knew he couldn't.

'If there was a feed bin out the back, maybe they had poultry,' she whispered.

'Or goats,' he said, abrupt because he was angry again, though trying not to show it. Angry because she was caught up in this mess—she who'd come to Tihoroa to escape buffeting emotions—seeking only peace and serenity as she awaited the birth of her child.

Tess nodded then motioned for him to come inside.

'It's no use guessing,' she reminded him. 'The blood samples will be in a lab tomorrow and maybe then we'll know for sure. Is there a specific test? Is it simple? Will we know anything as soon as tomorrow?'

He had followed her into the hut, his presence reminding her so much of the kiss they'd shared the previous evening she was all but shaking.

'There's a new test facilitator called an M-chip, not yet commercially available, but a lab in Brisbane has one for trials so, yes, we could know as soon as late tomorrow.'

'That would be good for everyone—it's the not knowing that makes everyone tense,' Tess said, adding, 'I've been wondering about encephalitis, with swelling of his brain causing the coma. Maybe viral or insect-borne. Aren't there some tropical strains of it?'

She saw his eyes twinkle and knew he was smiling behind the mask.

'I looked them up while I was researching bird flu. There are a number of possibilities and all of them are more encouraging from the islanders' point of view than bird flu, mainly because the worst of the encephalitis viruses are carried by mosquitoes but not the kind of mosquito we have here.'

'So now we're hoping my poor young man might have an infection that could lead to permanent brain damage, rather than the innocuous-sounding flu!'

He smiled again.

'Spot on!' he said. 'Which is why I'd better take some blood so we can confirm it.'

He headed for her bathroom, then poked his head back around the door.

'You are washing your hands thoroughly all the time, as well as wearing gloves?' he asked,

'Every time,' Tess assured him. 'It's an ingrained habit

with me, even with non-contagious patients. It's one of the first things nurses are taught in their practical work—hand-washing came before gloves and is still just as important.'

She thought this was a simple reply to an equally simple question, but Eduardo hesitated in the doorway, his eyes, above the whiteness of the mask, very dark.

Questioning…

Studying her…

Something of the intensity of that dark gaze shimmied down Tess's spine, and suddenly they were back where they'd been last night. The harsh words and accusations they'd exchanged meant nothing and the air was charged with the electricity that flowed between them.

Was it a second or an hour that passed?

Tess didn't know, standing transfixed by something beyond her control.

'Wash your hands,' she finally managed, and if the words sounded dry and strangled, that was because her throat was tight with the emotion still simmering in the room.

'I'd better,' Eduardo said, but Tess knew that didn't finish things. Right now they might have a desperately sick young man to care for, but somewhere, some time, there'd have to be a reckoning. This physical attraction between them would have to be put away once and for all, or maybe acted on.

Surely that would help it die…

She watched as he examined her patient, taking his temperature, blood pressure and pulse, although Tess had done it only fifteen minutes earlier, checking his pupils, going over his skin for any signs of a rash.

Then he picked up the chart Tess had been keeping.

'His temp's down, and his fluid output seems fine. I tested the blood we took earlier—we do simple blood tests here—and he was certainly dehydrated, his electrolytes all over the place, but I wonder now about continuing with fluids. If it is encephalitis, he should be on diuretics to remove fluid from his body and possibly ease the swelling in his head.'

'Is there a test for encephalitis?'

Eduardo nodded grimly.

'A test using cerebrospinal fluid, but I'm not practised enough to even attempt to withdraw some. One false move and I could cause leaking of the fluid and that would be far worse. Not that knowing will help much. If it's not an insect-borne type of encephalitis then it's been caused by some virus he's had and the blood test should show if there's been an infection, what it was, and how we should treat it. There are a couple of post-infection encephalitis strains that have specific treatments, but with the others it's a matter of keeping his temperature down so he doesn't suffer seizures, and maybe using corticosteroids.'

Tess shook her head.

'It's really too complicated for clinic medicine, isn't it? Can't we fly him to the mainland?'

Eduardo had finished his examination, and had put two vials of blood into a labelled plastic envelope. He nodded towards the door and Tess led the way outside, settling on the front step where he had waited for her that first day.

He passed her to sit on the ground the requisite three feet away, and pulled off his mask.

'When we send patients to the mainland, they are accepted on the basis that their stay there is temporary. But with our young man, the authorities over there are reluctant to take him in case, when he is better, we refuse to have him back.'

Tess stared at him.

'That's the most unfair thing I've ever heard. What about seamen who are ill at sea and have to be airlifted to the nearest country for treatment?'

Eduardo smiled at her vehemence. Here she was, no doubt exhausted after a very long and unexpected day, feeling anger towards her country for their seemingly uncaring attitude.

'Seamen have a country they can be repatriated to,' he reminded her. 'Most of the people here aren't willing to even name their home country, let alone be returned to it.'

'That's terrible!' Tess muttered, and he sensed rather then saw that her strength had finally given way. Moonlight shone on the tears that slid slowly down her cheeks.

Forget three feet of separation—this woman needed comfort.

He stood up and stepped towards her, settling by her side on the step, wrapping his arms around her and drawing her head down onto his shoulder.

'We cannot change the world,' he reminded her. 'All we can hope is that we make our little bits of it better.'

He felt her nod against his shoulder and tightened his arms, pressing his face against her soft hair, smelling the green smell—the freshness, the woman!

Tess!

'It's late, you should be in bed,' he said gently, hiding the desire that was rising in him again, burning in his body despite his own exhaustion.

'And so should you,' she murmured, lifting her head so she could look into his face.

The temptation was too great.

He kissed her.

A gentle kiss, almost a goodnight kiss, but the repressed attraction flared up once again, and the kiss became a searing acknowledgement of all that lay between them, strengthened by the fact they were so intent on denying it.

These thoughts flashed through Eduardo's head as he explored her skin, his lips on fire to learn her taste and texture, while his hands caressed her body and learned her shape, imprinting it into his mind so he knew he'd never lose his knowledge of it. He felt the swell of her belly, the heavy breasts, nipples tightening at his touch so they felt hard against his fingers. He felt her skin, satin smooth, cool to his slightly fevered hands, and the tangles in her long hair that tumbled so wantonly around her face.

'Tess?'

The word croaked from his throat, but this time it was she who was the strong one.

'I've a very sick man in the hut and a little girl in my bed,' she said, as she gently disentangled herself from his arms. 'So I'd better say goodnight. Sleep well.'

He stared at her, hearing the rebuff, knowing she was right but wanting her so badly he was shaking.

'Lila,' he said, his bewildered brain grasping at one small scrap of reality.

'Lila?' Tess echoed.

Eduardo stood up, anxious to get away and sort out his emotions—and calm his body down as well.

'The little girl,' he said. 'Her name is Lila.'

He took the blood over to the clinic, checked that it was carefully labelled, added a note to the envelope so the lab would know the patient's symptoms, then sat for a few minutes.

He could feel tiredness eating into his very bones, but his body recalled the feel of the woman in his arms while his mind remembered her bidding him to sleep well.

She wouldn't sleep.

At least, not properly.

His bet was she'd pull a chair close to the young man's bed and doze in it, too anxious about her patient to let sleep capture her completely.

And though every muscle in his body protested when he moved—pulling people out of the sea had tested most of them—he knew he had to return to her hut and take over the night shift, insisting she go to bed, no matter how much she argued.

He half smiled to himself, anticipating her argument, but as he walked back towards the hut his exhaustion lessened, a strange contentment creeping in as he considered spending a night under the same roof—in the same room, in fact—as Tess Beresford.

She was exactly where he'd expected her to be, slumped in a chair by the patient's bed, her feet resting on the side of it.

A bedside lamp had been left on so she could see her patient, if somewhat dimly, and so Eduardo saw her eyes widen when he appeared in the doorway.

'Didn't I tell you to go to bed?' he questioned softly as he slid off his sandals and padded quietly into the room.

'I can sleep like this,' she replied, her protest losing force as she whispered it.

'Not tonight,' he said, coming closer and lifting her feet off the bed, setting them on the floor then taking her hands to pull her up out of the chair. 'Tonight I'll keep watch over him. Tonight you sleep.'

Tess stood there, her hands warm in Eduardo's grasp, and shook her head.

'You really *do* worry about everyone, don't you?' she said quietly, then she lifted her hand and touched his silky black hair. 'But who worries about you, Eduardo?' she added, then she slipped away into the bathroom, returning minutes later to say thank you and climb gratefully into bed.

CHAPTER SIX

HE'D PUT HIMSELF in this position, Eduardo reminded himself for about the fortieth time as he heard Lila cry out in her sleep, and saw Tess roll over and wrap her arms around the little girl, drawing her into the warmth of her body.

Family!

That was what he'd sought.

What he'd expected of his life.

At first Ilse had protested they needed time together before they had a child, then later she'd refused because his work had been too important to him—too all-consuming— and she'd be left to raise the child or children on her own.

Now he sometimes wondered if there'd been other affairs.

If she'd put off motherhood so she could pursue her own interests.

And he, too, was to blame, for his work had taken him away from home for long hours, sometimes days on end, but when a breakthrough was possible—when success was hovering in the air above a Petri dish—how could he leave?

He tried to shake away the thoughts but they wouldn't be ignored. They'd been so close to a result in their research.

'Aaargh!'

His attention snapped to the young man on the bed, and

he reached out to hold the slender shoulder before his patient could try to rise.

'It's all right,' he said, as the young man, weak though he was, battled to sit up.

'Lila!'

The panic in his cry woke Tess, who sat up in bed and looked across at Eduardo. She sized up the situation in an instant and snapped on the bedside light, pulling back the sheet so the young man could see his sister.

He collapsed back onto his pillow and closed his eyes, and although Eduardo spoke to him, trying for a response of some kind, his eyes remained shut.

'Maybe he's sleeping naturally now,' Tess said, coming to stand on the other side of the bed and study their patient.

'Let's hope he is,' Eduardo answered her, grasping the young man's wrist and feeling the steady beat of his pulse. His breathing also seemed stronger, so maybe, just maybe, the crisis had passed.

'Do you think remembering his sister's name means there's no brain damage?' Tess asked, and Eduardo looked up at her, seeing for the first time how little her white cotton nightdress did to hide her figure, now backlit by the light behind her.

What had she asked?

He did a mental headshake and remembered.

'It could be a positive sign, but it could also be some survival mechanism—some instinct that prompted him to make sure his sister was safe before he plunged back into darkness.'

'Poor young man,' Tess said, then she raised her head and looked at Eduardo. 'You found out Lila's name, did no one tell you his? If we knew it we could use it when we talked to him.'

Eduardo gave a small shrug.

'I doubt the names we've been given for any of the adults are their real names. I think people who have been through what they must have suffered are ultra-protective of their real identities.'

Tess reached out and brushed the young man's arm, feeling the less hot skin—sure he was sleeping naturally now.

'I can understand that, but at least for him we've got Lila. Surely she will call him something when he wakes up again.'

'You're very positive about him waking up,' Eduardo teased, and she smiled at him, feeling all the twinges of desire but knowing this was something else. This was the tentative beginning of a friendship.

'I am,' she said, hiding the pleasure the thought gave her. 'And now I'm going to be equally positive about you leaving. I've had a good sleep and I'll take over. I realise it's nearly dawn but if you go now, at least you'll get some sleep too.'

He studied her for a moment, about to argue, she was sure, then he surprised her by nodding, standing up and walking away from the bed.

'You will put more clothes on before our patient wakes again,' he commanded, stopping in the doorway to strip off his mask.

Tess looked down at her white cotton nightie, which to her seemed to provide adequate coverage.

'It's a very modest nightdress,' she protested, and Eduardo grinned at her.

'Not when you've got a light behind you. It's a good thing I'm totally exhausted—or that we'd agreed an affair wasn't a good idea. Somewhere, there has to be an explanation why I didn't ravish you when I had the chance.'

He walked away, leaving Tess to run her hands over her body, wondering how he could be attracted to her in this condition—wondering also just how nice it would be to be ravished by Eduardo.

But he was right—they'd decided not to act on their attraction.

Hadn't they?

She settled into the chair by the patient's bed, then realised she was too far away if Lila cried again in her sleep, so she stood up and moved the chair to the other side. About to sit down, she remembered Eduardo's warning, so she changed her nightdress for a pair of very sensible shorts and a non-see-through top.

Then she sat down, pleased to have some thinking time, wondering just how an escape to Tihoroa had become so complicated.

She'd come to get away from family pressures—emotional pressures. Now here she was in danger of becoming emotionally entangled with a man who'd admitted he had nothing to offer her emotionally.

But wouldn't that be good?

As if!

No, the issue wasn't that Eduardo was emotionally bankrupt but that he saw himself that way. Tess had seen the love and affection he gave to all the islanders. The man was living, breathing emotion, rolled into a very sexy package.

She sighed, upset that she'd added the last bit to her thoughts. This was supposed to be an intellectual exercise, not an excuse to ponder Eduardo's sexiness.

Although it *was* undeniable!

OK, so her mind wasn't quite ready for sensible cogitation. She'd do the young man's obs, concentrate on him, and hope that whatever it was connecting her to Eduardo would go away on its own.

Lila woke up as Tess finished her check. The little girl looked around, her bottom lip trembling, and Tess hurried to scoop the child into her arms.

'See, he's getting better,' Tess said, carrying Lila close to her brother's bed. The young man must have heard her voice for his eyes opened and Lila kicked free of Tess's grasp and flung herself on the bed.

The young man put his arm around her, then his eyes closed again. Tess let the child lie beside her brother for a while, drawing comfort from him, then she mimed sleep with her folded hands beneath her head and lifted Lila off the bed.

The little girl seemed happy enough, especially when she saw the doll she'd found the previous evening. She picked it up and carried it across to the baskets and boxes of surprises, where she started going through them, eventually choosing a little red dress for herself, then a pair of shorts and a shirt which she carried carefully over and laid on her brother's bed.

'How long have you been looking after each other?' Tess asked, even though she knew the little one wouldn't understand her. But Tess's heart was aching with the love Lila was showing towards her brother.

Family!

It had its good points.

More than that, it was the basis of so much that was good and important in life and although Tess's particular family had been driving her nuts of late, she nonetheless felt a surge of gratitude towards them for their love and the lessons they'd taught her through their love.

But why would thoughts of family suddenly make her think of Eduardo?

She decided not to go there, busying herself instead in unpacking the donated items and stacking the clothing away in drawers, showing Lila which were hers and which her brother's. Then she had an idea and sat down on the floor with the little girl in front of her.

'I'm Tess,' she said pointing to herself. 'And you're Lila.'

Tess pointed to the child again, then repeated both their names until Lila pointed at her and said 'Tess' very shyly.

Tess clapped her hands to show her delight and hugged and kissed her, calling her by her name all the time. Then she pointed at the young man on the bed and repeated the pantomime of Tess and Lila.

She waited while Lila studied her, as if unsure this strange woman could be trusted with her brother's name. Then she stood up and ran across to take his hand and point to him.

'Hasim!' she said, and once again Tess told her how clever she was.

A call from outside told her someone had arrived with breakfast, and when Tess went out to take the tray that had been left on the step, she saw some of the other children playing outside, dancing around the shadows of the palm trees, their voices high and carefree, as if the stress of their escape and near disaster had already been put behind them.

Tess put out fruit and cereal and yoghurt on the table so her small friend could choose. She pointed to each item and giving it a name, laughing and clapping as Lila repeated them in her piping little voice. But when Tess made to serve her some of each, Lila took the spoon and bowl and carefully helped herself.

Was she older than she looked—which to Tess was about three—or had she been looking after herself for quite some time?

The thought made Tess look towards the bed, where she saw Hasim was again awake and smiling at his sister's antics.

'Would you like something to eat?' Tess said to him, miming eating with her hand, but Lila was ahead of her. No sooner had she seen her brother with his eyes open than she was by his side, her bowl and spoon in her hands, babbling to him in their own language, but unmistakably ready to feed him.

He took four spoonfuls, mainly, Tess was sure, to please his sister, but when he couldn't manage to open his mouth for a fifth, Tess gently led the little girl away, miming sleep again as Hasim's eyelids closed.

Lila finished the bowl and ate some more fruit, but she turned all the time to check her brother, and when Tess tried to tempt her outside for a breath of fresh air, she shook her head and took her doll and the little basket of shells to the foot of the bed where Hasim lay and played chatty games with these new treasures.

Tess ate her breakfast and was lifting the phone to call the clinic and report that Hasim had awoken up again and even eaten a little food when her call was forestalled by Eduardo appearing in the doorway.

'You haven't had enough sleep,' she told him, trying hard to hide her body's reaction to his appearance and annoyed that she hadn't had warning of his approach so she could put some protection in place.

'That's my part in this play,' he told her with a smile that made her feel lighter than air. 'I'm the one who's always telling you things like that.'

She smiled, although she knew she shouldn't.

'Well, today's it's my turn, but as you're here…'

She told him of Hasim waking up, and how they'd found out his name, and Lila feeding him.

It was her voice breaking on that last part that prompted Eduardo to come closer.

'It upset you, seeing it?' he asked gently.

She shook her head, but at his frankly disbelieving look she then nodded.

'I just hate to think what they must have gone through— and she's so little. Look, she's laid out clothes for him. What did a child do to deserve to lose her family, Eduardo? To have her childhood stolen from her?'

Eduardo wrapped his arms around her. He knew pregnant women were liable to get emotional, but somehow this went deeper with Tess. She was hurting so much for this child she barely knew, yet she too had known pain and loss.

Or maybe it was because of what she'd been through with her fiancé that she could so easily empathise with these strangers' lives.

He rocked her against his body—a friendly, comforting hug, nothing more.

And wondered again if what he felt was love…

It means nothing that he's wrapped his arms around me! He doesn't even want to get involved in an affair. He's just a really nice guy comforting an over-emotional woman.

Tess told herself all this as she stood in the circle of his arms, drawing heat and comfort from his body but desperately wanting more.

Was this how love felt? Wanting someone so much it hurt?

She couldn't remember that from her time with Grant

but, then, she'd always had Grant's love so had never had to yearn for it.

And she'd better stop yearning for this man's right now, because it was all wrong for so many reasons, not least of which was the fact that she was carrying Grant's baby...

The vague sense of betrayal this thought, as usual, brought in its train made her push away from the comfort of his arms.

'Thanks,' she said, in case he'd sensed more of her feelings than she wanted him to know. 'I needed a hug.'

She'd needed a hug! Eduardo backed away, nodded goodbye and strode towards the clinic. If ever there was a dampener to romance, it was a statement like that.

Romance?

Where did that come in?

Was it to do with this suspicion that his feelings for Tess weren't just physical?

Impossible!

He, who'd sworn never to love again?

Never to leave himself open to betrayal?

Fortunately, for his peace of mind, he heard the roar of engines overhead, which meant the plane was coming in. He'd grab one of the electric carts the company left around the canteen and take the blood samples out to the airport.

What he should do was fly out on the plane. A week away from Tess might help him get his feelings into perspective. But he could hardly leave with all the refugees there. But he *could* keep away from her. Now the young man was conscious, he might soon be well enough to be shifted in with some of the other refugees. He could avoid the clinic unless he was called in, and not do the island trips—in fact, it would be a good opportunity for him to get some serious work done in the lab.

Eduardo managed to avoid Tess for ten hours, but when the reports on the blood tests were rung through, he had to visit her.

'Your young man's had glandular fever,' he announced, stopping in the doorway to watch her reading a story to Lila—pointing to the illustrations of animals and saying the names then waiting for the little girl to repeat them.

'That's great news,' Tess responded, nodding towards the bed where the young man slept. 'So it was a complication of that and not anything more difficult to track down?'

She smiled her delight, but whether at his news or just at him, Eduardo wasn't sure.

What he was sure of was that he shouldn't be there. He could have sent Philippe to tell her the test results, then he wouldn't be standing in her doorway, lusting after her but also thinking those intrusive thoughts about family again.

Perhaps it was because his family, as in his parents and siblings, was so far away. He could go to Portugal—that's what he could do. Take a month, fly over, catch up with everyone. By the end of the month he'd be tired of the wrangles families always had and he'd be happy to return and she'd be gone.

He could even celebrate Christmas with his family and Tess would be nothing but a memory when he returned.

'Can we treat it?'

She was frowning now and he realised he'd been standing in the doorway, lost in his thoughts, for some minutes. Sorting out his immediate future. But Tess wasn't to know that.

'We keep treating him as we have been,' he managed to reply. 'Now he's conscious, it will just take time. We need

to see he doesn't overdo things as he starts to improve—
he'll need time to regain his strength.'

Tess nodded. She understood all that Eduardo was telling
her, yet the conversation had been strange—like talking on
the phone to someone in a foreign country where there was
always a bit of a time lapse before each person spoke.

'And the others? Does the line in the sand still remain?'

Instead of answering, Eduardo studied her for a moment.

'Does it worry you?' he asked.

She thought about her answer.

'Yes, because it segregates these people who have
already been through so much. I can't help but wonder if
they don't feel like outcasts—feel unwelcome. Yet I know
we have to do it, to keep them quarantined until we know
for sure they're not carrying some disease that could spread
among the islanders.'

She paused and in her turn studied Eduardo.

'I'm not very good with grey areas,' she admitted. 'I like
things black or white, right or wrong. I know that isn't the
way the world works, but I find life easier when I can
come down on one side or the other.'

He smiled at her.

'Which, I presume, is why you let family pressure get
to you. The people who wanted to take care of you weren't
doing anything wrong—in fact, they were being kind and
caring, which made it extra-hard for you to resist.'

She tried to shrug off this reading of her character, but
Eduardo was right, so instead she changed the subject.

'We're talking about the refugees, not me,' she reminded him.

'I think you'll find they're not too put out by the segrega-
tion. The islanders leave gifts of food and clothes and toys

for the children every day, and they stand along my line in the sand and talk to those guests who can understand English.'

'And the future?'

It was Eduardo's turn to shrug.

'The island council is holding meetings about it every evening, looking at all the options and trying to foresee possible complications. At the moment they are willing for the group to remain here in the islands, so are thinking about accommodation, and work opportunities, and whether difficulties could arise further down the track because of cultural or religious differences.'

'It's a huge undertaking—to offer them asylum here,' Tess said, and although Eduardo nodded, he also smiled.

'Historically the islands have offered asylum to many different nationalities, people jumping ship or put ashore as troublemakers, pirates who set up camps here. I think the mixed blood in the people makes them more liable to accept strangers because way back their ancestors might have been seen as equally strange.'

'Tolerance—it makes things easier all through our lives, doesn't it? If only we could all remember to practise it,' Tess whispered, and once again Eduardo felt the little catch in his heart that he knew had nothing to do with lust.

He said goodnight and walked away, mulling over the twinge, trying to explain it away so he could get his life back on track. He was a scientist so surely he could look at the situation from a scientific point of view. He'd look at cause and effect—or maybe effect and cause.

One, he was attracted to the woman but that was easily explained, given his recent celibacy and her beauty, both inner and outer. Two, he felt protective of her, but he'd worked that one out—it was her pregnancy. Three—well, three was the little catch—the twinge, the moment on the beach at Kiki…

Three was harder to explain away…

Perhaps if he set three aside and concentrated on getting over one and two, or at least keeping them under control, three would go away of its own accord.

For a start, he could avoid her. Now the young man—Hasim—was on the mend, he'd have no reason to keep calling by her hut.

Yes, avoidance was the answer. Not seeing her, not talking to her, not listening to the way her voice changed when she worried over something—that would at least contain numbers one and two.

But having settled on avoidance, why, two weeks later, when Hasim, though still weak, had insisted he and Lila move in with friends, when the refugees had been cleared of any contagion and were mixing happily with the islanders, and Tess was back on Mathilde's normal roster at the clinic, did Eduardo make a special trip to the clinic just to see her, then compound the error by inviting her to dinner?

'I know you're not on call, you've got the day off tomorrow to laze around, and young Lila's going to an islander birthday party this evening, so you've no excuse not to come to dinner then have a look around the lab when we've finished.'

She stared at him, perhaps surprised by the invitation when he had barely spoken to her about anything but medical matters for a fortnight. The lovely eyes were wary and they scanned his face as if trying to read his intentions.

'Colleagues sharing dinner,' he offered, and eventually she nodded, then her face brightened.

'Do I swim across with my going-out clothes in a plastic bag on the top of my head?'

'You could,' he said, smiling at the image, 'or I could pick you up at the jetty. Shall we say six-thirty?'

Say no, common sense shrieked inside Tess's head. This was right back where she'd started, shaking hands with pirates.

But she couldn't think of a single excuse she could use to refuse his invitation—he'd virtually covered them all before inviting her.

And saying, 'I don't want to' might sound petty and childish.

'Thank you,' she said instead, wondering just how much trouble she might be getting into.

A little after six she wandered down to the jetty, wanting to watch the sun set over the sea. A little way along a father was fishing with his children, baiting the hook for the youngest and casting out then letting him hold the small rod. The second child needed help attaching prawns to his hook but insisted he could cast, while the third, who couldn't have been more than six years old, was self-sufficient, baiting and casting proficiently, but glancing towards his father as he performed each movement for a nod of approval.

Watching them, the interaction of a father with his children, she couldn't help but wonder who would teach her child how to fish. If she had a boy, she imagined Dan or her father could take him fishing and teach him how to bait his hook and cast his line, but—

'You look pensive.'

Eduardo had come up behind her, and she pointed to the little family.

'Am I being selfish, denying my child a father? Can I do this on my own without depriving my child of something a father might provide?'

Eduardo smiled at her—a gentle smile.

'I thought the whole idea of coming to Tihoroa was to regain your confidence in your decision to have this baby and your confidence in yourself and your ability to handle single-motherhood.'

Tess returned his smile.

'You're right,' she said. 'And it has to a certain extent, as long as I'm not listening to any of the island women who are always telling me I need a man or watching a father teach his little boys how to fish.' She sighed. 'I guess even couples have doubts about their parenting abilities at times.'

'I'm sure they do, and I'm also sure that one committed parent is better than a family where the parents are at loggerheads all the time, or where one parent does all the parenting anyway. We've all seen children struggling in those situations.'

He put his arm around her shoulders and gave her a hug.

'You'll do the job brilliantly.'

It was a supportive hug, the hug of a friend, but as her nerves skittered with anticipation, she wondered again just how much trouble she might be getting into, visiting Eduardo in his home.

But all her fears were forgotten as she approached the house, climbing the stone steps from the jetty through a magical tropical wonderland. The sweet scent of frangipani hung in the air, and something even more potent—was it the ginger?—wove a spell around her senses. Flowers blazed with brilliant colour, purple, red, orange, bright pink—the colours of the sunset she looked forward to each day. Then she reached the top where a wide veranda stretched beneath a high-pitched thatched roof, and turned to look behind her.

The sea stretched for ever, it seemed, darkening now the sun was nearly gone, but she could still see the paler colours of the shallows, and the jades and purples that indicated reefs beneath the surface.

'It's beautiful!' She barely breathed the words, afraid to break the spell the beauty had cast around her.

'I miss the sunset but the sunrise over the water is equally spectacular,' Eduardo said, he, too, speaking quietly.

He led her along the veranda to where the sun would rise, and she could see small dots of islands far out in the placid water. Yes, the sunrise would certainly be spectacular to see, lying in the hammock slung between two poles or lazing on one of the lounges that formed a right angle adjacent to a low wooden table.

The tiny jolt of regret surprised her. It couldn't possibly be because she'd never see a sunrise from Eduardo's house. She was over all of that holiday romance nonsense. Not over the attraction she felt for him, but she'd done her pros and cons lists and knew that not giving in to it was by far the best option.

And he couldn't have been all that interested or he'd have taken her up on her original rather weak and feeble suggestion that they indulge in a brief affair.

He led her into the house—if it could be called a house. To Tess, it was more a huge, magical space. Wide wooden boards, painted white, made up the floor, while the interior walls were stone then plastered roughly over and painted white as well, but it was the roof that drew her attention. Round beams of golden bamboo held the thatch, each joining up in the middle with a much larger beam—the trunk of a coconut tree?—which ran along the highest part.

The walls on one side were lined to the roof with book-shelves stacked with books that looked well read. The large comfortable-looking lounge chairs were covered with fabric that had once been bright but had now faded to gentle reds and rich, dark blues and purples. They were set around more low wooden tables, and towards the back of the room was a huge dining table with at least a dozen chairs ranged around it.

'It's unbelievable,' she breathed, turning around slowly to take in all of the big open room and the views beyond to the blue of the sea and the darkening sky.

'It's home,' he said quietly, and she finally understood what kept him here in Tihoroa. He might miss the chal-lenge of working with his colleagues, but he'd fled back to this beautiful place when his work and his love had betrayed him, destroying all he'd believed in. And the house, the islands and the islanders had healed him.

Why would he want to leave?

The question caused another pang in Tess's heart, not unlike the one she'd felt when they'd talked of the sunrises.

Of course she couldn't stay here on Tihoroa. Number two item on her pro list for having Grant's child had been to give her parents a grandchild—both sets of parents in fact.

Although why she was thinking such daft thoughts she had no idea—Eduardo had no interest in her apart from an unlikely and slightly inconvenient attraction. Pregnancy must be addling her brain….

CHAPTER SEVEN

'COME, WE'LL EAT then I can show you where I work.'

Eduardo led her across the big room and out onto another veranda. From here she could see the rocky peak that she saw when she swam in the lagoon and realised the house was tucked up against its base.

'That is Rapuhepa, the guardian,' Eduardo said. 'Most storms and cyclones come from that direction so Rapuhepa protects the house.'

He had paused by a long table and was pouring drinks from a frosted crystal jug.

'Home-made lemonade,' he explained as he handed one to her. 'I don't make it. I am cared for—well cared for—by Ramon, who is Rose's son. He looks after the house and guesthouses when none of the family are here, and took me on as a special project when I returned. But although he made the lemonade and the salads, I am the cook tonight.'

He motioned towards a very modern-looking kettle bar-beque, from which delicious aromas were emanating.

'You like crayfish?'

'Crayfish? Like lobster?' Tess smiled her delight. 'Yes, I guess you could say I like it, although it's not something I buy each week on a nurse's salary.'

'Here it is free for the taking and these two I caught earlier today. Grilled with a little lime and some island spices, you will taste real crayfish.'

How could anyone have left him? Tess found herself wondering. He's thoughtful, caring, intelligent, fun to be with and—no, she wouldn't use the 's' word again...

She wandered to the edge of the veranda and looked at the broad-leaved plants that pushed up from the ground below. Tall stalks of creamy flowers, tinged with pink, told her where the strong, pervasive scent was coming from.

'Ginger flowers?' she asked, pulling one towards her to breathe in the perfume.

'They are,' Eduardo confirmed. 'A scent unlike any other, wouldn't you agree?'

Of course she agreed. She was so overwhelmed by the assault on all her senses she felt lost, in the nicest possible way. So lost in the strangeness of this tropical paradise, in its lushness and spectacular beauty, that she'd have agreed with anything.

Or almost anything...

Although that particular anything wasn't on offer. Eduardo was intent on being the perfect host—the kisses they'd shared forgotten as far as he was concerned.

What was on offer was a delicious crayfish and salads so exotic she had to poke around in them to try to identify the ingredients, many of which were unknown to her.

'Are all these fruits and vegetables native to the islands?' she asked, as she finally admitted defeat a little later and pushed back from the table with food still left on her plate.

'Of course not,' Eduardo told her. 'All the different nationalities that came here brought seeds or breeding birds and animals, some by choice but others by accident—a seed dropped from a piece of fruit, a couple of chickens escaping from a boat—who knows the origins? But now we have a mix of food from many nations.'

'Like you have a mix of people from those same nations,' Tess pointed out, leaning back to stretch her spine and allow both dinner and the baby room inside her abdomen.

Eduardo caught the movement and for the first time since she had arrived in his house saw her as a pregnant woman and not a woman he was lusting after.

'You are all right?'

She smiled at him.

'Very all right,' she said, 'although I should probably do four trips around your veranda to work off the dinner.'

'Come and see the lab instead,' he suggested, concern slipping away and leaving room for lust to return, but he cut it off. Doing colleague-type things would stop that nonsense.

He led her through the garden to where he'd built his lab. Like the guesthouses scattered through the grounds, he'd designed it as a smaller version of the big house, but inside it was all glass and stainless steel, a sterile space designed for work, not comfort.

Freezers and refrigerators lined one wall while the interior space was made up of benches with cupboards underneath and racks of equipment above them. Every surface shone with cleanliness, and the glass on the domed hood was free of fingermarks.

'Do you ever do any work here?' Tess asked, gazing around at the pristine equipment.

Eduardo laughed.

'Quite a lot lately,' he said, and she wondered if the words had some hidden message as his voice had deepened and he'd not looked at her as he spoke. 'I am lucky enough to have an assistant who's so proud to be working with me, he keeps the place spotless. Unfortunately, he's due to go to the mainland in the new year for his final years of high school then on to university, a doctor in the making. I'll have to find a new assistant.'

Tess moved around the room, afraid to touch the stainless-steel surfaces for fear of leaving fingerprints, stopping at the glass dome and peering into it.

'Those are my latest experiments—do you understand much about stem-cell research?'

'Only what I've read. I know there's great excitement over the possibility of eventually being able to use them to treat heart disease, diabetes, Parkinson's and spinal cord injury, and…'

She paused. Should she add the rest of her limited knowledge—the bit about the controversy of using human embryos to extract immature stem cells, which was what had led to Eduardo's court case?

He pushed a stool towards her and propped himself against a bench, arms folded across his chest.

'In Australia it is legal to use stem cells from embryos that were fertilised for IVF but were not used and are about to be destroyed. It is cloning human embryos for research that is the controversial issue.'

Tess nodded—it was more or less what she'd been about to say. Mind reading was alive and well on Tihoroa!

'In the laboratory where I worked, however, we didn't use embryos at all, preferring to use donated umbilical cords. As well as having stem cells in the blood in these cords they also have immature stem cells in the matrix— a thick mushy stuff that protects the blood vessels that pass through the cord.'

'But if this is available, why the fuss over embryonic stem cells?' Tess asked. 'Why cause a controversy and stir up ethical issues that people find hard to understand if there's no need?'

Eduardo smiled at her, making her feel warm and very nervous all at the same time. They were discussing science—she was interested in it—fascinated in fact—so why the tingle of attraction?

'A five-day-old embryo—a blastocyst—is like a little ball made up of one hundred and forty cells. The ones around the outside will form the placenta, while the ones inside will develop into the foetus. But at this stage those little cells don't know which of them will be brain cells, which bone, which kidneys, so, if harvested, those cells can be more easily persuaded to grow into whatever a scientist might want them to grow into.'

'Like bits of spinal cord or liver or whatever,' Tess said, following the explanation in spite of the tingle. 'And it's easier to trick them into growing into what the researcher wants because they haven't made up their own minds at that stage.'

Eduardo smiled at her phrasing but did agree.

'Exactly,' he said, 'but our work was focussed on what triggers the differentiation. In the UK some scientists working with colleagues in the US have fed stem cells from an umbilical cord with hormones and chemicals and have produced a very small piece of liver tissue. This mightn't seem very earth-shattering, but right now that little liver can be used to test drugs and eventually such research could lead to the production of whole livers for use in liver transplants. In other research umbilical cord stem cells have been made into neurons—brain cells.'

'It sounds earth-shattering enough for me,' Tess told him. She nodded towards the glass dome. 'So, what's cooking there?'

He smiled again.

'I've got some of Berthe's youngest's cord stem cells multiplying. That's the first stage. To get as many immature cells as possible so you have a supply to work on. We know how to persuade them to be nerve cells, but spinal cord cells are subtly different and it's how to tell them to be spinal cord cells that's my focus at the moment.'

'And wouldn't it be easier on the mainland? More babies, more umbilical cords, colleagues to discuss ideas with?'

Tess hadn't realised she was going to ask the question until it was out there in the open air—unable to be retrieved.

He looked at her for what seemed like for ever, then shook his head.

'A court case doesn't just affect your work, it strips your soul bare, Tess,' he said and turned away from her. 'Not only that, but it taints everyone around you. My ex-wife was kind enough to point that out to me before she left me.'

Let it go, her head warned, but her heart was aching for this wounded man. She went to him, touching him on the shoulder, forcing him to turn towards her once again.

'But you fought it and you won,' she protested. 'You proved the accusations false. Your laboratory had never worked with embryonic cells, let alone cloned ones. '

He smiled but it was such a poor effort her heart hurt even more.

'And how often do we see someone found innocent, sometimes on a legal technicality, and still have doubts? How often do we hear the name of someone who has been accused of something and even though found innocent we wonder if there was fire as well as smoke? Being found innocent doesn't defeat the doubters—it doesn't even satisfy the victim whose pride has been destroyed along with his or her belief in human nature.'

Tess was so angry she nearly stamped her foot.

'You can't possibly live among these islanders and not believe in the essential goodness of human nature, so don't give me that rubbish,' she snapped. 'And as for pride—don't we all take a pummelling in our pride from time to time? You hide yourself away out here, playing doctor and fiddling with your research when you could be doing far more effective experimentation, working with a team dedicated to the same result. OK, so you needed some time to put yourself back together again, I can understand that—it's why I'm here myself—but to stay here, that's just selfish.'

'Selfish?' he echoed, looking at her in such a bemused fashion she wondered if she'd grown another head. But she wasn't going to be put off.

'Yes, selfish!' she told him. 'What if my baby is born with spina bifida and needs some new spinal cord cells?'

He reached out and grasped her shoulder, his fingers gripping so tightly she flinched.

'Your baby? Spina bifida? It's shown up on a scan? Is that why you're here? You needed time to think it through? To readjust? Oh, Tess!'

He wrapped his arms around her and held her close, warming and comforting her with his body—seducing her with kindness, although he didn't know it.

Tess felt her anger ebb as she realised the depth of his concern for her and her unborn child, but she couldn't take false comfort. She pushed out of his arms and laid her palm gently on his cheek.

'My baby's fine,' she told him. 'That was just a "what if" scenario.'

Dark eyes met hers but whereas he and most of the islanders seemed able to read her mind, she could read nothing of his mood in his eyes or fathom the thoughts behind that intent regard.

'I'll take you home,' he said quietly, and she felt a totally inappropriate surge of disappointment. Though why would he want her in his house when she'd abused his hospitality by being rude to him—by virtually accusing him of moral cowardice, she didn't know.

She wanted to apologise—wanted him to suggest coffee on the eastern veranda looking out over the sea—wanted him to hold her in his arms again and kiss her with the hunger she'd felt in him before. But here he was, leading her back to the house then through it, picking up a fringed and beaded shawl off a hat rack near his front door, wrapping it around her shoulders in a detached, impersonal way, warning her at the same time that it would be cool on the boat.

He took her arm to guide her down the steps, ready to steady her if she slipped, and if her heart felt as if it had cracked open and was now seeping blood, that was her problem.

Back at the main jetty a little later, he tied the small boat securely and insisted on walking her home, his closeness making her nerves itch with desire, while his total detachment chilled her to the bone.

'Thank you,' she said, when, after what had seemed an interminable walk, they reached her front step. 'It was a lovely dinner.'

Apologise, one voice was yelling at her, but she didn't listen to it, feeling she'd been right to speak out as she had.

She began to unwrap the shawl from around her shoulders to return it to him, but the tasselled fringe must have caught in her hair.

'Let me,' Eduardo said, stepping closer, lifting his hands and threading his fingers into her hair to untangle the fringe. He smelt of the wind and the sea and ginger blossoms and barbeque and man. Tess breathed it in then whispered his name, and the kiss that hadn't happened earlier became inevitable, his lips just brushing hers at first, then closing on them, claiming them, forcing them open so his tongue could invade her mouth and take fiery possession of her senses.

His hands slid through her hair, spreading it around her shoulders, the shawl falling unheeded to the ground. And when kissing wasn't enough, he lifted her, carrying her effortlessly up the step and into the hut, setting her back on her feet, but close by the bed so the backs of her knees were pressed against the mattress.

'I have tried to resist you,' he growled into her ear, while his thumbs brushed across nipples already peaked to meet his touch. 'This is not right—we both know it. You are a sexy, vibrant woman and you need a man in your life—a father for your baby as well—but I am not that man, Tess. I am little more than the pirate you first thought me, shipwrecked by love and now ready to take satisfaction where I find it. You understand that?'

His hands were fondling her over-sensitive breasts and an ache that only sex would heal was burning between her legs. But she needed to make sense of what he was saying, didn't she?

Maybe not!

Maybe they were back where they'd been when they

first kissed and she'd more or less suggested they could have an affair.

But now she loved him!

The thought shocked her so much she stopped kissing him, stopped her hands caressing the warm, silky skin on his back, but he took it as a different signal, easing her back onto the bed then lying down beside her, intent on bringing pleasure to her with such expertise she couldn't breathe, let alone tell him to stop.

Then gently and with such tenderness she found tears rolling down her cheeks, he made love to her, curled behind her so she felt only pleasure, not discomfort, fondling her and whispering sweet endearments while he transported her to heights she'd never realised existed, splitting her body apart with sheer sensation that burned and quivered through every cell.

And afterwards he lay with her, still holding her, so she slept in a man's arms for the first time in her life.

Secure.

Safe.

Loved.

No, maybe not loved, she realised dreamily as she tucked herself closer to the warmth of his body, but a facsimile of it that would do for now.

For tonight…

He was gone when she woke up the next morning, not, a note beside her bed said, because he wanted to leave, but because he didn't want the islanders gossiping about her. He'd see her later, the note continued, but that was it. No word of love.

'Why would there be, you daft female?' Tess demanded

of the empty room, but she couldn't feel angry, her body slack with the exhaustion pleasure brought, and warm with memories of that pleasure.

'Tess?'

Lila's tentative cry made Tess sit up and pull on a nightgown before calling to the little girl to come in, holding out her arms for the child's good-morning hug. It was a routine begun when Hasim and Lila had moved in with their friends, this good-morning visit and a hug, followed by an English lesson as Tess rose and washed and dressed, explaining every move she made in English, with Lila repeating the words.

Only today Lila was ahead of her, going to the small cane dresser and picking up Tess's hairbrush.

'Brush,' she said proudly, carrying it over to the bed and beginning to pull it through Tess's hair. Unable to stand the pain for more than a few minutes, Tess diverted her by pointing to a new book Rose had brought in the previous day.

'Let's read,' she suggested, taking the brush and hurriedly removing the worst of the knots in her long hair before Lila returned. Then she lifted the little girl onto the bed and they began to read.

Eduardo heard their voices—Tess saying words and Lila repeating them in her bird-like voice—as he approached the hut. He'd not swum across today, deciding instead to arrive at the main jetty at a time when a lot of people were about to see him. He'd gone to the canteen, explaining to the staff it was Tess's day off and getting them to make up a tray of the things she liked to eat for breakfast. He'd even put a Thermos of weak coffee on it, knowing how much she appreciated the treat first thing in the morning.

So now he was hovering outside her hut, the tray growing heavier in his hands, jealous of a motherless little girl who was no doubt snuggled up in bed with Tess.

'*Stupido!*' he muttered to himself, then he stepped up onto the veranda, calling out to Tess to warn her of his approach.

'Come in,' she called back, but he doubted there was any more warmth in her voice for him than when she'd called to Lila.

He shook his head, aware he was behaving like—like what? A lovesick fool? He, who'd vowed never to fall in love again?

But it wasn't love—it was desire. Like a man lost in the desert finding water and needing more than one drink, his recent celibacy made him want more than one night of love with Tess Beresford.

He made his way slowly into the room, nodding his head in confirmation of his own thoughts when he saw the child snuggled against Tess's side.

'As it's your day off, I brought you breakfast,' he said, sounding so stiff he could have been a butler in a very posh hotel.

But if his voice was giving nothing away, surely his eyes were, for they were caressing Tess's body as his hands had the previous night, and his mind was remembering—his body remembering...

'That's so kind,' she said, and sounded far more together than he had. 'Lila's just come for a visit so she can share it.'

She hesitated then smiled at him—a shy, slightly embarrassed smile that hit him like a stab wound in the heart.

'And you?' she asked quietly. 'Did you bring enough for you to share it with us?'

What could he say? That of course he'd brought enough for two? That he'd imagined a different 'us'?

That he'd thought breakfast in bed might lead to other bed pursuits…

Fortunately, before he got himself into an even worse mess, he heard the plane engines thrumming overhead. He put the tray down on the end of the bed, trying not to look at the rosy flush that made her nipples visible through the fine cotton nightdress.

'There's plenty there but I won't stay, I wanted to meet the plane today. Apparently there's a visitor coming in and as all the visitors' huts are occupied, I want to offer him one of the guesthouses at my place.'

'That's kind of you,' Tess said. 'Is it a pearl buyer?'

She'd been there long enough to know that they were the most frequent visitors, although a range of people, from appliance salesmen to zoologists, also used the huts.

'You know, I didn't think to ask,' Eduardo said, and Tess had to smile. He'd been looking so confused since he'd walked in she'd guessed he hadn't expected to see Lila in the bed. And though his note had said he didn't want to draw attention to her, bringing her breakfast in bed and then staying to share it with her would surely have done just that.

Thank goodness for the plane and the visitor arriving. At least now, when Lila went back to play with her friends, Tess would have a chance to sort out how she felt about the situation. Something that would have been impossible with Eduardo in her hut…

Or in her bed…

The visitor was tall, with blond streaks in his brown hair, clad in casual slacks and a polo shirt, smiling and laughing with a couple of local women as he came down the steps of the plane, carrying a colourful woven basket that obviously belonged to one of the women.

The other woman saw Eduardo and began to wave and point, then led the visitor towards him.

'Eduardo, this is Mr Alderton—he is here for Tess, to see her and to marry her, he says. So her baby *will* have a father after all.'

Both women clapped their hands to show their delight at this outcome, while nausea boiled within Eduardo, so much so it took him a moment or two to realise the visitor was offering his hand.

And his name.

'Dan Alderton,' he said. 'And the marrying Tess part isn't quite sorted yet, although I'm sure she'll see the sense of it in the end. It's why she wanted to get away for a bit— to think it through.'

Eduardo shook hands automatically, although his primal instinct was to kill the man. Then an echo of one of his early conversations with Tess returned.

Dan! The baby's uncle? Did he love Tess or was this a duty he felt he had to undertake?

For the baby or for Tess?

It had better be for Tess—she'd see straight through an offer made from patronage.

'Welcome to Tihoroa,' Eduardo managed, then he remembered why he'd met the plane. 'We're fresh out of visitors' huts at the moment, but you're welcome to stay at my place. In fact, that's why I came out to the airport today. I'll take you there so you can settle in and freshen up after your journey then later I can show you where Tess lives.'

And you'll have to swim across every time you want to see her!

The ungracious thought made him feel small, yet slightly better at the same time. And the man didn't protest at the plan and insist on seeing Tess first, a situation Eduardo would have foiled somehow, knowing she was probably still in bed, all rosy from their—

Dio! What had he—they—done?

The man—Dan—had retrieved his luggage, a sensibly sized duffel bag, and was standing expectantly beside the buggy.

Eduardo took the bag and threw it in the back then ushered Dan into the front seat. He drove towards the main settlement, pointing out things of interest as they passed.

'The sorting shed for the pearls, eh?' Dan said as they passed the shed. 'I'd like to look through that if it's possible. Tihoroan pearls are making a big splash all over the world these days.'

'You are interested in jewellery?' Eduardo asked, and Dan shook his head.

'But I'm interested in business and any business that does as well as Tihoroan pearls is worth a look.'

Would *he* have wanted to look at pearls if Tess was on the island? Eduardo wondered, stopping the buggy at the end of the jetty and pointing to his boat.

'You reach your home by boat?' Dan queried. 'Is it on another island? I understood Tess was here, on the main island.'

'She is, and my island is joined by the reef to the main island. You can easily swim across, or take the boat or jetski to get back and forth.'

Eduardo hesitated, then an emotion he didn't want to investigate prompted him to add, 'Though you'd best do the trip in daylight a few times before you try it at night.'

Dan began to protest that he was putting Eduardo out, but Eduardo had grabbed the bag and was leading the way along the jetty to where his boat was moored.

It was the behaviour of a jealous lover, this keeping Dan and Tess apart. He realised that, yet couldn't seem to stop himself. Dan seemed familiar with boats, casting off forward and aft without being asked, then standing beside Eduardo as he piloted it home, asking about the make of the boat, guessing the length correctly, checking the engine size.

'You live here permanently?' he asked and though Eduardo opened his mouth to say yes, he found himself prevaricating.

'I've always had a home here and have been back for a year now, but permanently? I don't know.'

'Do the islands have another doctor if you leave?'

Eduardo was bringing his boat in at his jetty, and could have avoided answering, but the question was polite 'guest talk' and he was racked with guilt over what had happened last night, so he explained, 'It would be easy enough to get one—in fact, we've a couple of islanders already qualified, doing intern and resident work and getting experience, one in the U.S. and one in Australia, but the clinic is staffed by competent nurses who can manage, with the Australian flying doctors on standby for serious cases.'

'I was worried about Tess coming to such an isolated place, pregnant as she is. We all were, her family and mine. But knowing there was a doctor here made it easier.'

More guilt clamped around Eduardo's conscience, but something in the way the man spoke raised a whisper of doubt in his mind.

'Worried for Tess or the baby?' he asked as Dan disembarked and Eduardo tossed his bag up to him.

'Well, this baby's pretty special,' Dan replied. 'Did she explain about Grant? It's my brother Grant's child she's carrying so, as you can imagine, my parents are very anxious about it. And about Tess, of course.'

Tess as an afterthought! One bump and I could push him into the water...

'It's why I want to marry her. Not that she's not a great girl—'

Girl?

'But the baby should be an Alderton and have all the advantages of the family name and be included in the distribution of the family's wealth. He should follow in his father's footsteps at a private school, whereas Tess is intending to bring him up on her nurse's salary, even refusing financial help from her parents, who can well afford to keep both her and the baby. It's ridiculous that the boy should be deprived of anything.'

'You speak of a boy—are you so sure of that?' Eduardo asked, leading the way up the steps as fast as he could in the hope of showing up Dan Alderton's fitness.

But the man kept one step behind all the way and wasn't even breathing hard when he reached the top and answered Eduardo's question.

'Aldertons always have sons. There hasn't been a girl born into our family for generations. Strong sperm, we always say.'

He smiled at Eduardo as if he expected a doctor to appreciate his little joke, but Eduardo was contemplating pushing his guest back down the steps, although he knew that wasn't the best behaviour for a host.

He showed Dan through the house, trying not to think of Tess's presence in it the previous night, then led him through the gardens to a guesthouse, introducing him to Ramon, who was cutting back a strand of miniature bamboo beside the ornamental pond.

'If there's anything you need, there's a buzzer near the front door that will bring Ramon to the guesthouse. There's a swimming pool quite close, and if you go back around the house you'll find a path leading down to the lagoon. It's quite safe to swim there.'

Dan expressed amazement at the beauty of the small abode, and gratitude to Eduardo for making it available, then spoke with genuine pleasure of the beauty all around them. Eduardo found himself warming to the man.

After all, he was trying to do the right thing by Tess, bringing her into his family. The importance of family was something most Portuguese understood. And from the outside, looking in, it seemed an admirable solution. The baby would have a father, Tess would have a man to take care of her—although if Dan had any sense he wouldn't phrase it quite like that—and they would be a family, tucked into the larger families of Aldertons—all male—and Beresfords.

Maybe, if he could get over his murderous urges and set aside the guilt weighing down his conscience, he could help Dan promote his suit—help Tess see that this was the perfect solution for her. After all, it had only been last night that she'd been fretting over not having a father for her baby.

So Dan Alderton was the perfect solution—the complete package—a husband and a father rolled into one.

While he himself could go back to his solitary hermitage here on the island…

Couldn't he?

* * *

With breakfast finished, Lila went off to play with friends. Tess got out of bed, stretched and did her exercises, then showered and dressed in her swimming costume. She packed some fruit left over from breakfast into her beach bag, along with sunscreen, a towel and a book.

She had a day off and she was going to spend it at the lagoon, resting in the shade, swimming when she found herself getting too hot, and generally relaxing.

Physically at least. Mentally her brain was going at a mile a minute, replaying the previous evening, from the moment she'd walked into Eduardo's house, through the harsh words she'd flung at him in the laboratory, and then…

She stopped at the part where they'd got back to her hut, although physical memories took over then, causing little ripples of remembrance through her flesh.

'Eduardo!'

She whispered his name as she walked through the palm trees towards the lagoon, and heard the swaying fronds above her repeat the word. *Eduardo, Eduardo,* they whispered, until the name was all around her, as his arms had been last night.

She knew it was impossible.

Even if he loved her, how could she live here, paradise though it was? She was having this baby for herself, but other people had rights to know and love it, and the baby had the right to loving grandparents, so staying on Tihoroa just wasn't an option.

Now, go back to the 'even if'! She knew damn well Eduardo didn't love her—he'd told her that. Emotionally bankrupt, he'd said, and she could understand that.

So the 'staying on at Tihoroa' wasn't going to be an option she needed to consider.

She reached the lagoon, found a shady spot and spread

her towel on the sand. She sat down on it to spread sun protection on her skin, and looked across at the rocky island.

Rapuhepa—she knew the name of the rocky outcrop now. The guardian.

But who would be her guardian? Her rock?

Not Eduardo—that was for sure....

CHAPTER EIGHT

EDUARDO LEFT HIS guest at the house and headed for the lagoon, stripping off his clothes and plunging into the cool water, needing exercise to blot out his thoughts.

Back and forth he swam, long, strong strokes, setting himself challenges, freestyle up and back, then butterfly, breaststroke—a stroke he hated—then freestyle again.

Finally tired enough to take a break and tired enough to have numbed his mind, he stood up in the shallows—the main island shallows, not his own shallows.

Tess was sleeping on the beach—and had obviously slept through all his splashing and exertion. Lying on her side, one hand under her head, the other curled protectively around her belly, she was oblivious to his presence.

Oblivious, too, to the sun that had crept higher in the sky so her feet were now in sunlight.

He walked up the beach, his footsteps all but soundless in the sand, and draped her white shirt across her legs and feet. A feeling of protectiveness swept over him, so fierce he wanted to sit nearby and watch over her as she slept.

Because she looked vulnerable?

It must be that. It certainly wasn't voyeurism for all he felt was…

What?

He didn't want to think about it too long so went back to being protective. He told himself no harm would come to her and she'd wake before the sun crept further up than her legs and, thus reassured, he walked back down the beach to plunge into the water yet again.

His visitor would be showered and dressed, ready to see the woman he wanted to marry. Eduardo pulled on his shorts and trudged back up to his house, trying to make sense of the various dilemmas Dan Alderton's arrival had caused.

Given that Dan was one of the reasons Tess had fled to Tihoroa, wouldn't it be right to warn Tess that Dan was here?

On the other hand, seeing the unexpected meeting might have some value. If she flew into her baby's uncle's arms, then he would know—

'Know what?'

'Pardon?'

Ramon was hovering at the top of the steps, and his question made Eduardo realise he'd been thinking aloud. Hopefully only the last thought had escaped as he wouldn't have liked anyone to hear the others.

'The visitor is ready to go to the main island to see his friend.'

From the careful way Ramon phrased the sentence, he obviously realised he was treading on delicate ground.

So much for keeping Tess safe from islander gossip!

'I'll take him across, Ramon,' Eduardo told him. 'And show him around the place when we get there. We'll probably have lunch in the canteen but I'll bring him back here for dinner, so if you could think about something local we might eat…'

Ramon didn't question this suggestion, although

Eduardo's conscience did. Was he making these arrangements to keep Tess and Dan apart? Particularly at night when sweet tropical breezes and a huge moon hanging like a Chinese lantern above the sea made romance all but inevitable?

Quelling his conscience with a reminder that Tess *had* included Dan in the list of people she was escaping, he continued on to the house where he found his guest waiting on the front veranda.

'This must be as close to heaven as you can get,' Dan greeted him, waving towards the blue water, dotted with rocky outcrops of islands large and small, the pristine white beaches and the coral reefs, now at low tide, visible just beneath the water. 'How come developers haven't discovered it? It's an ideal place for a really exclusive holiday resort—you've got a runway big enough to handle executive jets and if they built cabins similar to your guesthouses, even the fussiest of wealthy tourists could find no complaints.'

He didn't wait for Eduardo's answer, continuing, 'And speaking of the guesthouse, that hand soap and body lotion you have in the bathroom—excellent products. Are they locally made? Would whoever makes them be interested in an export contract?'

Eduardo listened to this conversation with a feeling of disbelief. Wasn't the man here to persuade Tess to marry him? If so, how could he be thinking of tourism and soap?

But Eduardo was the host, so he answered the queries, leading the way down to the boat at the same time.

'I think the islanders believe they have enough without tourism. Even eco-tourism can bring more people to an area than the area can responsibly handle, while as for the soap and creams and other toiletries in your bathroom, that's a cottage industry begun by some of the women. If and when they feel ready to export their products, they'll have advice and support from the pearling company, which is doing a very good job of their own export business.'

'Ah, a closed shop?' Dan said, following Eduardo down the steps. 'That makes it more of a challenge. But I have to agree with you about the expertise Tihoroan Pearls has as far as marketing is concerned. They've done extraordinarily well. Could we perhaps see their offices and sorting room this morning?'

'I thought you were here to see Tess?' Eduardo couldn't help saying.

'Of course I am, but she's probably working. I can catch up with her tonight. The truth is, we didn't part on the best of terms, mainly because I pushed too hard and she can be a very stubborn woman when she wants to be, but the weeks she's had here, I'm sure, will have persuaded her my idea is the best way to go.'

'Your idea?'

'Marrying her, of course. I thought I'd explained that earlier. How many divers does the company employ? And how often do they dive? Has anyone ever done a cost-effectiveness survey on the workforce? One of our companies was recently able to take forty people off the payroll, just by using different work methods and offering incentives for those willing to work longer hours.'

He was casting off the mooring ropes as he explained this great innovation to Eduardo, who wondered if there would ever be an incentive strong enough for islanders to spend less time with their families.

Yet this man talked of family, linking Tess to the conversation, and Eduardo had been persuaded by his talk.

And realistically speaking, Tess had admitted wanting a husband and family but in fourteen years she hadn't found anyone to love. This was where arranged marriages were good, and if a marriage were to be arranged, Dan was obviously the perfect choice for her.

Tess woke up with a fuzzy, slept-too-long feeling and stretched carefully. The sun had moved high enough for its warm rays to reach her knees. Had she been thinking clearly enough to have covered her legs with her shirt before she'd gone to sleep?

She shook her head, unable to remember, but was glad she had.

Stretching again, she felt her muscles loosen, and found herself smiling as she looked across the lagoon to Eduardo's island.

'Smiling about what?' she asked herself, speaking out loud because there was no one about.

But even asked out loud, the question couldn't raise an answer, although she kept smiling.

Maybe it was just the memory of sheer physical pleasure, she decided, rubbing her hands up and down her arms, then across her belly, feeling the baby move inside her.

Should she think about last night? Think about what it might—or might not—have meant to Eduardo?

Better not—she'd go with baby names. Beatrice, Bella, Bryony was nice, not Beverly or Barbara, although they were sure to come back into fashion one day, and it was no use, even if Eduardo did have feelings for her, because she couldn't bring Bridget up so far from her grandparents.

Unable to believe Eduardo had crept back into her mind

when she was so busy with baby names she stood up, stretched again and walked down to the water, working her way through the Cs now—Caroline or maybe just Caro, Chrissie, Charlotte, that was a good name…

She swam across the lagoon, pausing in the shallows, tempted to go up to the house, but held back by the insecurity of not knowing what would happen next between herself and Eduardo.

So she lay on the warm sand for a few minutes, Eduardo's sand—how pathetic could a woman get?—then swam back, playing in the deeper water for a while, exercising her legs and enjoying the feeling of weightlessness when Charlotte was getting heavier each day.

Yes, maybe Charlotte was right, although only going as far as the Cs seemed to be cheating the baby of what could be better possibilities.

Finally, with her legs tired from treading water and her mind numbed by baby names, she made her way back to shore—her shore—and let the sun dry the water off her so her skin felt tight and tingly with the salt that remained on it.

Showers always felt so much better when there was salt to be washed off.

Clean, refreshed and clad in her sensible shorts and a fine cotton shirt, she considered a plan for the rest of the day. With Christmas fast approaching—the day after she returned home—maybe today would be a good day to buy some Christmas presents. The company had a small store selling pearls and locally made pearl jewellery as well as soaps, scents and lotions some local women made.

She'd buy a pearl ring for her mother and a pearl pendant

for Mrs Alderton, then soaps and body lotions for her friends and work colleagues back home. Maybe some pearl earrings for herself—a memento of her time on Tihoroa.

Intent on this plan, she failed to notice there were other customers in the shop until a gasp that was ill concealed as a cough made her turn her head. Eduardo, pretending still to cough, and—

'Dan? What on earth are you doing here?'

The tall, handsome man straightened from his inspection of some jewellery and turned towards her.

'Tess!' he said, making his voice deep and velvety, as only he could do. 'Oh, darling, you look ravishing. I know pregnant women are supposed to glow, but you—the world could bask in the warmth of *your* glow!'

He stepped forward and wrapped his arms around her, and Tess, too dumbfounded by his presence to move, stood unresisting as one hand tilted her face towards his.

He's going to kiss me and Eduardo is standing watching and what the hell is going on?

She moved her head in time for the kiss to hit her cheek, then put her hands against his chest so she could push herself free.

'Dan?' Repeating his name seemed to be all she was capable of doing, then she remembered where they were and found the question she'd asked earlier.

'Why are you here? What's happened?'

Now panic struck.

'Mum and Dad? Has there been an accident?'

It was Eduardo who reached her first, taking her arm and guiding her onto a stool at the side of the shop. Had he realised her knees were shaking? That her legs were barely strong enough to hold her up?

'Your parents are OK, Tess,' he kept repeating as he sat her down. 'Dan just came to see you.'

But the moment of panic had left too much emotion in its wake, and Tess began to shake.

'You stand here beside her, reassure her,' Eduardo said to Dan. 'I'll get some brandy.'

'She's pregnant, she shouldn't drink alcohol,' Dan reminded him, coming to stand beside Tess and putting his hand proprietorially on her shoulder.

'And I'm her doctor,' Eduardo snapped, although that wasn't altogether true. Tess, with Janne's help, had been doing her own weekly tests, and didn't know he'd been monitoring all the results so he could pick up the slightest hint of anything going wrong.

He found brandy in the company board room and poured a little into a glass, asking one of the secretaries to make a cup of tea as well, and bring it to the shop.

'I'm feeling quite all right,' Tess protested when he handed her the glass, but he could see how pale she was beneath her tan and see the tremble in her fingers, although she had them clasped to hide the evidence of shock.

'Just sip it,' he ordered. 'There's tea coming as well. Did you get some lunch? You know you've got to keep up the calories at this time.'

She took three sips of brandy then handed him back the glass, being careful not to let her fingers brush against his in the exchange.

Or had he just imagined that?

'I'm fine now, and don't need tea, but I do need to eat. You're right, that's probably it. I spent too long at the beach.'

She looked up at Eduardo as she spoke and her eyes seemed to be pleading with him for something.

But what?

To not mention last night?

As if he would!

'I was just about to take Dan over to the canteen. I've got a buggy outside—he can drive and you can point the way.'

'You'll join us there?' she asked, and he realised that had been the message she'd been sending. *Don't leave me alone with Dan.* But why? Because he'd nag at her about single parenthood? Did she know he wanted to marry her?

Eduardo could make sense of none of it, but he'd join them in the canteen—against his better judgement.

Why hadn't he flown out on the plane—gone home to Portugal for a month or so?

He joined them in the canteen, pleased Tess had chosen a table in a corner rather than the one they frequently sat at, which looked out over the beach and water.

Pleased?

He must be losing his mind to be *pleased* about such a thing. The sooner he got back to civilization, the better. Maybe a laboratory in Portugal…

'Glad you could join us,' Dan greeted him when they had all returned from the servery with plates of food and were about to begin eating. 'You can help me persuade this stubborn woman that her baby needs a father.'

Eduardo stared at the other man in disbelief. If this was the way he'd asked Tess to marry him the first time, it was no wonder she'd refused. And no wonder Dan Alderton was still single, if a chat over lunch with another person present was his idea of a romantic proposal.

Eduardo shifted uncomfortably on his chair.

The 'stubborn woman' was looking at him with a 'well, go for it' expression on her face, daring him to join in this conspiracy against her. Dan was smiling good-naturedly, totally oblivious of the tension thrumming in the air around them.

Still, there was a lot to be said for marrying Tess off to her baby's uncle. Other children would have the same blood, and though the thought of Tess producing this man's children made Eduardo feel physically sick, he knew that once Tess was married, he'd be safe. Maybe lost for a while, but he was used to that. He'd had a bad enough experience himself to know he could never get involved with a married woman—and even thinking about her could be termed as involvement, especially the thoughts he'd been having.

He looked at his lunch companions, both watching him expectantly, then took a deep breath and declared his loyalty, not to Tess but to Dan.

'You *were* worrying about not having a father for the baby just yesterday,' he reminded her, speaking gently because it hurt to say the words.

She stared at him, disbelief so vivid in her eyes it seemed to flash like lightning across the table.

'Thank you Dr del Riga, but when or *if* I decide my child needs a father, I'll choose one myself, not rely on traitorous colleagues or persistent relatives. I'm sorry, Dan, but the answer is still no, so it's going to be a long week for you on the island.'

Dan's shrug showed little in the way of devastation that Tess had turned him down. In fact, it seemed as if he'd expected it, but it was his reply that stunned Eduardo.

'Oh, I won't be here a week. I've got a charter plane coming in tomorrow to collect me.'

Tess rose to her feet and glared down at the man.

'You came all the way up here, thinking a quick proposal was all that was needed to have me falling at your feet? You didn't even plan to stay to talk about a wedding or to kiss me and walk on the beach in the moonlight and maybe find out if we were suited to each other in other ways than you being Grant's brother? You had it diarised, did you? Friday, fly up to Tihoroa, propose to Tess, fly back Saturday in time for— What's happening on Saturday, Dan? Squash or tennis?'

'It's actually a board meeting and this was very inconvenient, if you must know!' Dan snapped. 'And it's all very well, you running off to a desert island, but you've left a lot of very concerned people behind.'

'Rubbish!' Tess told him. 'I email my parents every day and phone them once a week, and I email your parents every week as well.'

'Well, you wouldn't have had to be emailing them if you'd stayed at home. This is just typical of your selfish behaviour, like getting pregnant without telling anyone, without even consulting my family.'

'So, had we married, Grant and I were supposed to have consulted you all before we made love each night? Is that what you're saying?'

Her face was flushed and she looked truly magnificent but Eduardo was concerned her blood pressure might be rising dangerously high. He too, stood up and put his hand on her arm.

'Tess,' he began, speaking gently, but it was obviously the wrong move for she turned her fiery gaze on him.

'And as for you,' she growled, brushing off his hand as if it was an annoying fly. 'Just where do you get off, putting in your two cents' worth?'

She gave them both a fulminating look, muttered, 'Men!' not quite under her breath, and marched out of the canteen, only aware the whole scene had been avidly followed when all the women clapped her on her way out.

Eduardo studied the spurned suitor, wondering if any man could have made a worse hash of things than Dan had.

'Can you stay a little longer—maybe talk to her alone? It probably wasn't the best idea, bringing up marriage over lunch, with someone else present.'

Dan glanced at him, his attention momentarily diverted from his meal.

'But Tess knows it would be a marriage of convenience. We like each other well enough, although you might not guess that from her performance just now.' He paused, then added, 'I assume it's the pregnancy making her so volatile. She's normally a very placid woman.'

He doesn't know her at all, Eduardo thought, but at the same time he could still see the sense in the arrangement Dan was proposing.

'I think women like a bit of romance in a proposal, even when they're not pregnant,' he said, although the thought of this man walking with Tess in the moonlight was making him clench his teeth hard to prevent a protest from slipping out.

Dan looked up again, chewing thoughtfully.

'You're probably right. Do you know what the dressing is they use on this salad? It's delicious. Aldertons are thinking of going into a line of salad dressing, getting a high-profile actor or sportsperson to front them.'

Eduardo sighed. Much as he would like to see Tess safely married off to someone, that someone wasn't this man. He was so focused on business matters that he'd kill her soul…

The siren interrupted his gloomy thoughts and stopped all chatter in the canteen.

'Excuse me,' he said to Dan. 'I'm needed at the clinic.

I'll send someone to act as a guide around the island or to take you back to my place.'

'The siren means trouble?'

'Big trouble!' Eduardo replied. 'A diving accident of some kind. They are rare, fortunately, but until we know for sure what happened, the clinic staff are all needed.'

He walked away swiftly, thinking now of the emergency, Dan Alderton forgotten.

Almost forgotten. The first person he saw in the clinic was Tess, talking on the radio to one of the boats.

She signed off as he watched and turned towards him.

'It's on board the *Nymbus,* a diver with decompression sickness. I didn't ask how it happened, but when he came up he was OK then he got dizzy and confused as they were coming in. They should dock in three minutes.'

Eduardo glanced out the window and saw the diving boat approaching the jetty, and Janne and Philippe waiting there with a wheeled stretcher.

'Have you used a hyperbaric chamber before, or seen one in use?' Eduardo asked, and Tess, the altercation in the canteen forgotten as she worried about the incoming patient, nodded.

'Not for decompression treatment, but I've seen one in use for sportsmen and -women who've had injuries. Hyperbaric therapy is used quite regularly now to promote healing.'

'You know the dangers?'

Tess knew he had to ask, because an untrained person adjusting atmospheric pressure in the chamber could do more harm than good.

'There's a risk of fire with the oxygen levels pumped so high, and for the patient risk of pulmonary damage, which is why we limit time within the chamber to a maximum of ninety minutes each session.'

Janne and Philippe were racing down the jetty, a couple of men from the boat running beside them, keeping the trolley steady.

'Poor man. Think of those little bubbles of nitrogen trapped in his tissue and joint spaces—the pain it must cause,' Tess whispered.

Then the patient was there, and while the sailors dropped back, Janne and Philippe wheeled the young man into the room where the hyperbaric chamber awaited him.

But this wasn't the simple, comfortable chamber used to treat sports injuries, this was a state-of-the-art machine that looked more like a large spacecraft. She'd never been inside this room as it was kept locked, and now she could see why, for the equipment in it must have cost a fortune.

'It's huge,' she said.

'It can take two patients at a time and a nurse attendant. Marianne should be here shortly—she's the expert—although Philippe is pretty good as well.'

Eduardo snapped out orders for blood pressure, pulse and respiration measurements to be taken, at the same time sliding a cannula into the patient's wrist and taping it, ready to supply fluid or medication when it was needed.

He was asking questions of the patient but getting little response.

An older man had appeared in the doorway.

'He was diving at about twenty metres, Eduardo,' he said. 'When he came up he was fine, laughing and joking, then as we were coming in he became confused, his breathing funny, and he said he felt dizzy. Do you think it's the bends or an air embolus?'

'Both are treated the same way initially,' Eduardo told the worried man. 'But the delayed reaction suggests decompression sickness. Perhaps he came up too fast, or went deeper than he realised and used the tables for twenty metres to rise. However it happened, we'll get him back under pressure then monitor him there.'

Marianne, a nurse Tess had met only once as she'd been on holidays, arrived and began speaking rapidly to Eduardo, then the entry door on the chamber was opened and the pair of them lifted Reuben in, still on his trolley.

'They can leave him on the trolley or shift him to one of the beds,' Philippe explained to Tess, 'usually depending on how much time he'll spend in there. See, we can watch through this porthole.'

He led Tess to the side of the metal contraption where she could indeed watch through the porthole.

'The hatch here is where we can pass in medicines, or meals, or small things that might be needed.' Philippe continued to explain the workings of the chamber to Tess. 'It has two doors so the atmospheric pressure in the chamber doesn't alter too much when the outer door is opened.'

Tess watched through the porthole as Marianne and Eduardo lifted the patient onto a bed, then began attaching tubes and pads and monitor lines to him.

'The monitor gives us constant blood pressure, ECG and oxygen saturation readings, with screens both inside the chamber, so the patient and nurse can see them, and outside, for whoever is monitoring things out here. On the other side is a ventilator for whatever gas mix they need to use and a scavenging system to prevent oxygen build-up.'

With Reuben apparently settled, Eduardo appeared to have some final words with Marianne, then he left the chamber and he and Philippe sealed the entry door and checked all other portholes and vents were closed.

'Because we think he was deeper than eighteen metres, we need to decompress him to the equivalent atmosphere of twenty metres. The air in the chamber is a normal air mix of 21 percent oxygen and 79 percent nitrogen, but once we've taken them lower than eighteen metres, the nitrogen can act as a narcotic on the brain and make things worse, so we use a mix of helium and oxygen. Reuben will breathe that in for thirty minutes then take a break while we reduce the atmospheric pressure in the chamber to the equivalent of eighteen metres then go onto thirty-minute sessions of pure oxygen until we reduce him down to nine metres when he can have an hour of oxygen with longer breaks between the doses.'

Through the porthole, Tess watched Marianne fit a helmet, not unlike a clear plastic spaceman's helmet with a soft collar, over the patient's head and attach two tubes to it.

Eduardo adjusted the dial on the chamber. Tess understood they would have to apply the same atmospheric pressure as the diver had been in when the trouble had begun, but the talk of helium was new to her.

'Helium? Like in the balloons?' she queried.

It was Janne who answered, smiling at her.

'Just like the balloons, and they come out with the same squeaky voices as you get if you inhale from a helium balloon.'

'The problem is, if we give more oxygen to balance the effects of the nitrogen, it can lead to oxygen toxicity, as well as adding to the fire risk. Normal oxygen saturation in the blood is 0.3 millilitres of oxygen to every 100 millilitres of blood, but we can take that up to almost 6 millilitres per 100 millilitres when we're treating decompression sickness.'

Tess realised Eduardo was explaining this for Janne and Philippe as well as for her, which meant such accidents must be rare. She watched the monitor screens, intent on the young man's well-being within the chamber.

'Is he still in pain?' she asked Eduardo, when Janne and Philippe had returned to their normal duties and the man she'd taken to be the *Nymbus*'s captain had returned to his boat.

'Yes,' Eduardo said, peering through the porthole on his side of the chamber. 'But not as severe and that will stop shortly, then we can decrease the atmospheric pressure at regular intervals as if we were bringing him slowly towards the surface.'

'And the air embolus?' Tess asked, interested in this new aspect of medicine.

'That happens more often when a diver goes down too fast and the pressure of the water squeezes the lungs and one of the tiny air sacs splits and allows a bubble of air into the blood. This can travel anywhere but if it goes into one of the carotid arteries, it can block flow of blood to the brain.'

'Oh!'

'I think that's the less likely scenario,' Eduardo said. 'These men are very experienced divers. Even the younger ones have been swimming and diving since they were children. Reuben is a daredevil and a competitive one at that. My guess is he wanted to beat some record for pearls and stayed down too long then panicked when he realised he was out of air in his tank. We'll get him right.'

'You keep him here rather than fly him out?'

Eduardo smiled at her.

'We definitely don't fly him out—in fact, we don't like the divers flying for a few days after their last dive. Once you're up in a plane the atmosphere gets lighter and although commercial flights are pressurized, the atmosphere in them is still lighter than air so for a diver who might have a few bubbles of nitrogen left in his body, this causes the same problems as surfacing too fast.'

Tess nodded, then turned back to the monitors. But now she was reassured that the diver would eventually be all right, she became aware of Eduardo. Not Eduardo the doctor, or even Eduardo the interfering colleague who had so infuriated her at lunch. But Eduardo the lover, who had given her such delight the previous evening.

She glanced his way, but if he was feeling any ripples of attraction they were well hidden.

And why would he be?

He'd made love to her, sure, but there he was, less than twenty-four hours later, trying to marry her off to Dan. Oh, he'd never denied the physical attraction between them, but apart from that she meant nothing to him.

And it wasn't as if he hadn't said as much to her several times…

Frustrated with the track her thoughts were taking, she sighed.

'You don't have to be here,' Eduardo told her. 'It *is* your day off. I could get Janne in to watch the monitors.'

'I don't mind staying—I wasn't doing anything else,' she said, her voice as carefully casual as his had been.

'Are you hiding?'

That made her turn to face him.

'Hiding?'

Dark eyes hid his secret thoughts—if he had secret thoughts. His face was as bland as a melon.

'From Dan?' he said, and she felt the fury that had built up at the lunch table launching through her once again.

'I do not need to hide from Dan,' she said, spacing each word out so he couldn't miss the message.

He shrugged, then very quietly offered his opinion yet again.

'It still makes sense to me,' he said. 'You marrying Dan, I mean.'

Tess just stared at him, speechless, but also deeply hurt…

CHAPTER NINE

DAN DEPARTED THE following morning, more upset about
not getting a contract to import soaps and lotions or per-
mission to build an exclusive resort on Tihoroa than by
Tess's refusal to marry him.

Or so it seemed to Tess as she drove him to the airport
to meet his charter flight.

This assumption proved right when he kissed her
goodbye—a formal kiss on the cheek.

'Well, I'll see you next week. If I can't get to the airport
I'll have someone pick you up. We'll talk again then.'

'Talk about what?' Tess asked, amazed he couldn't see
the smoke of her fury coming out of her ears.

'Why, getting married, of course!'

'Get on the plane!' she ordered through gritted teeth, and
as he walked towards it she got back in the buggy and
drove, too fast, back to the settlement.

Fortunately, the little electric vehicle's top speed was
only about twenty-five kilometres an hour so she wasn't
putting anyone at risk.

Except herself and her baby, she decided when she
jolted over a bump and banged her stomach against the
steering-wheel. She slowed down to barely faster than a

walk, although driving slowly wasn't as good an outlet for her anger as speeding had been.

She parked outside the canteen and walked across to the clinic. Sitting watching the dials on the hyperbaric chamber couldn't possibly upset her and might even soothe her temper.

But Eduardo was there before her, not watching the dials but talking to Reuben.

'I've done a full examination of him and although I think he might need another session in the chamber, we'll let him have a break,' he said to Tess.

'Can I take a shower?' Reuben asked.

'With Philippe nearby in case you feel dizzy. And you'll be staying here at the clinic overnight again,' Eduardo told him. 'I know you well enough to guess you're probably not feeling nearly as well as you make out you are.'

Reuben offered him a slightly shamed smile.

'Maybe not quite as well, but I really need a shower.'

'I'll get Philippe,' Tess offered, anxious to be away from Eduardo, but escape was impossible as he followed her out of the room.

'You saw your friend off?' Too bland the question but Tess met bland with bland.

'Yes.'

She found Philippe and asked him to stay with Reuben while he showered, then checked the clinic lists to see if anyone was coming in for an appointment.

Saturdays were usually slow, so she wasn't surprised to see the page was bare.

'You don't have to stay—Philippe's here, he can call you if he needs you.'

Now that he'd spoken to her, she had to face Eduardo.

'I've nothing else to do, so I may as well be here.'

'That is a terrible thing to say—nothing else to do! Have you snorkelled here? Out over the reef? No, of course you haven't. The tide's just right. Come on, let's get you kitted out and I'll show you the real beauty of Tihoroa.'

He took her hand in a friendly grasp and led her out of the clinic.

I should let go, Tess told herself, but her fingers wouldn't move and holding hands with Eduardo felt so good—so safe—she felt her anger ebbing and her nerves settling down.

But she couldn't allow herself to think about how good the hand-holding felt—where was she up to with her baby names?

They went into the little shop where Eduardo insisted on paying for a mask, snorkel and pair of flippers for her. Then he commandeered a buggy and drove them both to the lagoon, stopping long enough at Tess's hut for her to change into her swimming costume and grab a towel and shirt.

'You've used a snorkel and mask before?' he asked, handing her the new purchases when they reached the beach.

'Back in the swimming pool at home when I was six or seven.'

'Did you have long hair then?' he asked, and she looked up from adjusting the strap on the mask, bemused by the question.

'I was picturing you as a child,' he said, then he waved across the lagoon and Tess saw Ramon standing there, black swim gear in his hands.

'You can practise with the mask and snorkel while we swim across,' Eduardo said. 'The best coral bommie is over on my side. You know bommie?'

'I may have heard the word,' Tess said cautiously, wondering what she was getting herself into. She sat down on the sand to pull on her flippers.

'It's really bombora—a huge lump of coral, like a rock. Bommie is the word divers use. Other corals grow around it and fish flash in and out of the caves and through the branches of the staghorn corals. We have giant clams there, and sea anemones so big they could swallow a whole fish. Do you know they sting—sea anemones? It's how they subdue their prey. Only it is too weak a toxin to affect us.'

'Which is all fascinating,' Tess said, 'and I'm dying to see it, but now I've got my flippers on I very much doubt I can stand up. It's something to do with having penguin feet and a bulging belly conspiring to ruin my centre of gravity.'

Eduardo laughed and took both her hands to tug her to her feet, then held her elbow as she clumsily flapped her way down to the water. But once afloat the rest was easy and she found herself breathing naturally through her snorkel, her eyes following the brilliant-coloured little fish that darted through the water beneath her. She flipped her legs with casual ease, the flippers providing extra momentum, and soon saw the sand sloping upward, a warning they were near Eduardo's beach.

Not wanting to be cast on the sand again, she stayed in the water while Eduardo donned his gear. Then he joined her and once again took her hand, only this time it was to guide her towards a hidden paradise. Her first sight of the bommie, a huge lump of brain coral, made her gasp so she had to cough water out of her snorkel, but she easily fell back into the rhythm of breathing and they moved slowly over the coral mass, Tess marvelling at the bright blue of the starfish that clung to the rock, the pinks and purples of the staghorn coral, the vivid red of a fragile-looking species, and the pink fans of what looked like delicate lace but once again was coral.

Beneath them were the giant clams, sunk into the sand of the seabed, their upper fleshy lips dark blue and green and purple, velvety and soft-looking, so tempting for a fish to stray within their grasp.

And everywhere were fish, striped, red and white with long dainty spines along their bodies, jewel colours in the tiny species that darted through the tentacles of the anemones. It was magic and fairyland all rolled into one.

The tug on her hand reminded her she had a companion and she turned her head towards Eduardo, who was pointing towards the beach.

She let him lead her back to shore—to his beach.

'You mustn't stay too long, you'll get more tired than you realise,' he said, holding up a towel Ramon must have left and wrapping it around her before easing her down onto the sand.

He knelt at her feet and slipped off her flippers, and her heart, which had almost ached with the beauty that had been on offer in the water, now ached in earnest.

She loved him and he didn't know, and even if he did it would make no difference. Eduardo saw himself as tainted by his past and was too honourable a man to allow a woman to be tarnished by his reputation.

With her flippers off, he sat back on his heels and looked at her.

Was it because he had read her thoughts again that he was frowning?

'I can understand you being upset by Dan's casual proposal and his behaviour in insisting you marry him,' Eduardo said, showing just how far from reading her thoughts he'd been. 'But is it just Dan or does the whole idea of a marriage of convenience repel you?'

Tess stared at him, unable to believe they were having this conversation. But he'd asked a question and she knew he'd asked it out of concern for her, so she gave it some thought before she answered.

'I think I can see a lot of sense in a marriage of convenience in certain situations,' she began cautiously. 'In fact, although Dan comes across as crass and so business-oriented you want to scream, he is a kind man and would be a good and faithful husband and in other circumstances, yes, if I decided my baby needed a father I would have married him.'

Eduardo looked more confused than she'd felt when he'd asked the question.

'But you won't? Because of circumstances?'

His frown had deepened and he looked more perplexed than ever.

'Oh, for heaven's sake,' Tess snapped. 'I can't marry Dan because I love someone else.'

There, it was out.

Well, some of it was out.

'A marriage of convenience is all very well if both the partners are heart-whole and fancy-free. There's even a chance they'll fall in love with each other. But to go into such an arrangement when one person is already in love with someone else, well, that would be disastrous. It would be cheating, if only in the heart. It would be…' She couldn't think of a word strong enough, so finished with a weak, 'Unfair.'

She was in love with someone else! The idea hit Eduardo with the force of a bit of meteorite spinning down to earth from outer space.

The man she wore scarlet underwear for—it had to be.

But why wouldn't *he* marry Tess?

He was married already?

It had to be that!

'I'll just have a swim,' he managed to say. 'Ramon brought a picnic basket down for us. There's water and juice in there, and sunscreen. Make sure you don't get burnt.'

Was he really uttering these inanities to Tess?

He must be for she was looking as perplexed as he felt, but he had to sort out his own feelings before he could offer help to anyone else.

Particularly to Tess…

Tess watched him stroke cleanly through the waters of the lagoon. 'Well, that went down well,' she muttered. 'Tell a man you love him and he dives into the water and swims to another island!'

She had to smile at the image, seeing the situation as a cartoon in her head. But the heat of the sun reminded her she needed sunscreen and her body needed fluids. She scrambled to her feet, pleased now Eduardo wasn't there to see her ungainly movements, and walked up the beach to where Ramon had left a picnic basket and more towels and even some beach chairs in the shade of a pandanus palm.

She was drinking water when the first pain struck. A stomach cramp because the water had been too cold. But, no, it was a different cramp. False contraction—she must be due to start having them. Braxton-Hicks' contractions they were called—low down in the abdomen. She breathed in and out, not quite certain where the pain was. Walking—that's what you did for Braxton-Hicks' contractions. Walk them off.

Clutching the bottle of water in her hand, she began to

walk along the beach. Eduardo had reached the other side of the lagoon and no doubt would soon return. Best if she had the pains sorted out by then. He'd only fuss.

They did ease as she walked but didn't entirely disappear. Perhaps if she rested…

She spread a towel in the shade, took a bunch of grapes from the picnic basket and lay down, closing her eyes so she could recall the vivid colours of the underwater wonderland, drifting towards sleep.

'Yeow!'

The cry burst from her lips before she could wake enough to hold it back, and she curled on her side, hoping to contain it—to make it go away.

Panic fluttered in her chest, although she tried desperately to hold it at bay. The baby was thirty-four weeks, far enough along in its development to be safely delivered. Everything would be all right. Eduardo was here.

She uncurled enough to look around.

He wasn't here at all.

In fact, he'd turned and was swimming back towards the main island, oblivious to her cry and her pain.

It would go away. All she had to do was breathe.

In, out, in, out, keep it even, the pain would go.

And it did.

Almost…

She uncurled and sat up, ready to signal Eduardo when he swam back this way.

If he swam back this way…

But then blood came, staining the towel on which she sat, and terror—for the baby, not herself—gripped her.

'Eduardo,' she screamed, and saw him stop swimming. She yelled his name again and now he turned and churned back towards her, the slow, perfect strokes giving way to splashing haste.

'Tess?' he cried, racing up the beach towards her.

'Pains, Eduardo, and bleeding. And it's my fault—I drove the buggy too fast and hit a bump. I've hurt the baby!'

'The baby will be fine—they're used to bumps,' he assured her as he took in the situation. He looked up at the steps that led back to his house and considered going up those steps then back down to the boat. But the boat would jolt Tess too much as they sped towards the main island. So, not the boat. It would be better to...

'I'm going to swim you across. The buggy's on the other side—it's the fastest, safest way. Just lie back and keep breathing. You'll be all right, I promise, Tess. You'll be all right.'

But the desperation in that promise worried her more than the pain, which had receded once again, so she didn't answer, simply allowing Eduardo to lift her in his strong arms and carry her into the water, floating her on her back while he held her with one arm and backstroked swiftly across the lagoon.

Once on the other side, he carried her up the beach, stopping to get her towel and wrap it around her, before putting her gently into the buggy.

'Hold on if you can,' he said. 'I'm going to push it.'

And so for the second time in one day Tess was racing in a buggy beneath the palm trees. Only today they weren't whispering Eduardo's name—today they were saying, *Hurry, hurry.*

Once at the clinic he carried her straight to the little theatre, pausing on the way to ask Philippe to get Janne right away.

'I'm going to examine you first,' he said to Tess, gently removing her swimsuit and tossing it aside, covering her with a clean sheet. 'You're how many weeks?'

'Thirty-four,' she managed, as the pain swept through her once again and only her grip on Eduardo's hand served to anchor her.

Janne came in and began the regular checks while Eduardo gently disengaged his hand for a physical examination.

'Your cervix isn't dilating so they are not normal contractions.'

Tess managed a weak smile.

'Just how rare did you tell me abruptio placentae is?'

The attempt at a joke hurt Eduardo almost more than the pathetic smile had, but he couldn't let Tess know just how worried he was.

'At least I've had practice,' he joked back, pressing gently on her abdomen and feeling her flinch in pain.

'FHR slowing,' Janne said, and he watched Tess close her eyes, willing down the panic she must be feeling, willing the baby of the man she'd loved so long ago to be all right.

But Eduardo couldn't let himself think about Tess—not Tess as Tess. This was a patient in trouble and he was the only person who could help her.

He put a cannula in her arm and started fluids, adding a mild sedative so she'd need less anaesthetic when Janne put her under. Philippe had joined them, having found another off-duty nurse to come in and watch Reuben.

'I'm going to operate,' he told Tess, knowing she should be signing consent forms but not wanting to upset her any more than she already was.

She nodded, then said, 'Yes, please,' in such a quiet

voice he wanted nothing more than to take her in his arms and comfort her.

But saving her life and that of her baby took precedence, so he checked they had everything they needed, nodded to Janne to begin the anaesthetic and with a quiet prayer to any god who might be listening, he began.

The baby *was* a girl, something that seemed to upset a very woozy Tess far more than he could believe. He'd been sitting by her bed when she woke up. He was holding the baby, who was breathing well on her own, in his arms so he could show her to Tess as soon as she opened her eyes.

But though she smiled and held out her arms for her daughter, then smiled again as she examined her, there was distress in her voice when she spoke.

'A girl! I'm only up to the Ds and I haven't really done any of them because Dorinda of all stupid names kept rattling in my head.'

Eduardo could make no sense of it and, deciding his patient was still not fully conscious, he put a protective hand beneath hers as she held the tiny girl.

'Ds?' he ventured, hoping to clarify the subject.

'With names!' Tess said impatiently. 'I quite like Charlotte but that doesn't seem fair, to call her that without checking out the rest of the alphabet.'

'Oh!' Eduardo said, because there didn't seem to be anything else to say in this situation. Except there was!

'My mother's name is Charlotte,' he offered. 'Well, our version of it—Carlotta.'

Tess looked at him and tears slid down her cheeks.

'May I have it? May I give this little one your mother's name? I needed a connection so badly. It will have to be the English version or she'll forever be having to spell it for people and explain it's Portuguese.'

Eduardo stared at her.

She was crying because he'd given her baby his mother's name?

It had to be a hangover from the anaesthetic because the Tess he knew was strong and independent and so centred she certainly wouldn't get weepy over a name.

He watched her, now unwrapping her baby, checking fingers and toes, counting them, as new mothers had surely done right down through the ages, and wanted her as he'd never wanted anyone or anything before. Not just physically, but the whole package—the woman and the baby.

Family…

But what could he offer them?

A life on Tihoroa when he knew full well what this baby meant to two families on the mainland?

Or a life back there, with a man tainted by suspicion? A man who'd already failed at marriage?

CHAPTER TEN

'I'M USELESS HERE, I should go home,' Tess complained to Rose, who'd appointed herself as Charlotte's nurse or nanny or special guardian and had brought the baby in for Tess to cuddle.

'You can't go home,' Rose told her bluntly. 'You're not well enough for this week's plane. Maybe next week. You'll be home just after Christmas and with a late Christmas-present baby to show your family.'

Tess blinked back tears of frustration, though why she was always crying she didn't really know. Except that she *was* frustrated. The infection that hadn't materialised with Berthe had certainly found her, and for the three days after the dramatic birth she'd been too sick to care what was happening to her. Then too weak to argue with all the people who were telling her what to do—for her own good, of course.

Chief among these had been Eduardo, appearing at regular intervals by her bedside, giving doctor's orders, acting like a doctor, as remote as the steppes of Russia. Although a couple of times she'd heard a murmuring by her bed at night, and had lifted one eyelid to see him sitting there, her daughter cradled in his arms, his voice a whisper as he talked to Charlotte, telling her about the mother who was too weak to hold her and too full of antibiotics to feed her.

Telling Charlotte nice things Tess didn't know Eduardo knew, like how sometimes when she was thinking, she used both hands to lift the weight of her hair up, holding it on top of her head with bits of it spilling down everywhere, and how she always went into the cold water of the lagoon very slowly, walking in so the water crept up her body bit by bit.

And she'd go back to sleep with Eduardo's voice in her ear and her baby nearby and in the morning not be sure if it had all been a dream.

He'd also been keeping in touch with her family back home. Rose had told Tess that the previous evening.

'He had your mother's phone number on your job details and as soon as Charlotte was born he phoned her to tell her about the baby then he got the number for baby's other grandparents and tells them and gets email addresses for both families, and now he sends pictures every day.'

'Every day?'

'She changes and they like to see.'

Eduardo was sending pictures of the baby to her family and the Aldertons?

Why should he care?

Because he knew from Tess how much this baby meant to them?

She'd shaken her head in disbelief...

Now Rose was back, though not with mind-blowing information this time—just with the baby.

'Can I at least start feeding her?' Tess asked, as the little flower face nuzzled against her heavy breasts.

'Eduardo says tomorrow. He's been talking to a paedia-

trician on the mainland and he says tomorrow all the antibiotics should be out of your system and the infection as well.'

'What if it's too late—if I can't feed her?' Tess asked, as
the insecurity of being so useless brought worries in its wake.

'You give her bottle. Plenty of babies brought up on
bottles with no ill effects at all. Mother's milk is very good
and very convenient as you don't need fridge or micro-
wave, but baby formula is good these days so don't worry
about it. Don't worry about anything!'

'As if!' Tess muttered, thinking of her family and the
Aldertons back home, getting plenty of emailed pictures
of their grandchild but champing at the bit to see her.

But taking Charlotte home meant leaving Tihoroa, and
leaving Tihoroa meant never seeing Eduardo again,
which, all things considered, was probably for the best,
but that didn't lessen the ache in her heart whenever she
thought about it.

Damn, but she had to stop this weepy thing. She was
better than that and she knew only too well that most tears
were tears of self-pity and she didn't do self-pity.

She took a deep breath and concentrated on her baby.
Charlotte had been sleeping, but now her eyes opened and
slowly focussed on Tess's face, and love surged in where
self-pity had been, filling so many of the empty places
inside Tess that she knew she'd make it.

Oh, she might hurt for Eduardo for a while but all hurts
lessened in time, and now she had this little person to love
and care for, she'd have little time to brood over a love that
could never have worked.

So now, for the first time, she really looked at Charlotte,
studying the pudgy baby features, thinking how impossible
it was to see resemblances in babies. Oh, he's got your

eyes, people said to new mothers, but how the squinty baby eyes could show a likeness was beyond Tess.

But what she did know was that this was Grant's child, so she started telling Charlotte about her father, little things like the cow's-lick he'd had at the front of his hair so it wouldn't ever sit the way he wanted it to, and about his dog called Butch, which had followed him everywhere.

'We could have a dog called Butch,' she told Charlotte. 'Maybe not a cattle dog like Butch the first, but something small and fluffy, and people would wonder why we called a little fluffy dog Butch, but only we would know.'

She rocked her child against her and more tears fell, while outside the door an eavesdropper was swallowing a huge lump in his throat.

Eduardo had come to tell Tess she could start breast-feeding, but now he wasn't sure he could face her without giving away just how much he loved her.

He'd let Rose tell her about the breast feeding…

Eduardo hadn't been in all day, frustrating Tess who had so badly wanted to tell him about Charlotte's first attempt at breastfeeding and how good it had been for both of them, and that maybe Charlotte already understood some things Tess said to her. But most of all she'd just wanted to see Eduardo— to grasp every possible minute she could have with him, even in a patient-doctor way, before she left him behind for ever.

He'd come for sure at sunset, she thought as Rose wheeled Tess and the baby out to see the glory of the daily magic, but although Lila sidled up beside the wheelchair for her third visit of the day, Eduardo wasn't there.

Where is he? she wanted to demand of Rose, but she knew she couldn't. Love was the pits!

She'd been thinking about that when she'd fallen asleep later, so it was strange to wake up to find the man she loved once again sitting by her side.

'I'm sorry to wake you,' he said, touching her gently on the shoulder. 'But Rose said you wanted to do the night feeds so I brought Charlotte in to you.'

'*You* brought Charlotte into me? What are you doing here at night? Is there an emergency?'

He'd turned on a nightlight and now, with the baby held securely in one arm, he helped Tess sit up, raising the back of the bed to give her support.

'I've been helping out,' he said, then must have realised just how pathetic that sounded and added, 'Actually, I've been doing her night feeds. We don't ever get a baby without family here so it was a good opportunity for me to do some baby stuff. I can bath her and change her and she likes her bottle just a little bit cooler than Rose says babies usually like it.'

This information was so close to incomprehensible that Tess just shook her head. Charlotte was nuzzling at her nightgown in search of a midnight snack, so Tess settled her comfortably against her body and helped the little mouth find the nipple.

The greedy sucking started a reaction in Tess's body that made her shiver. She knew the reaction was to help her abdominal muscles tighten after the stretching they had received during pregnancy, but they were the same muscles that tightened with pleasure during sex, and with Eduardo sitting there…

'Does he know you love him?'

The question, coming out of nowhere, was so bizarre Tess turned to stare at the questioner.

'Does who know I love him?' she demanded blankly.

'The man you love,' Eduardo explained, adding patiently, 'The scarlet underwear man?'

'The scarlet underwear man?' Tess repeated, even more bamboozled but glad at least they were off the subject of the man she really loved.

'You were wearing sexy scarlet underwear the day I rubbed your back, and I figured women only bought that kind of thing for men, so there must be a man, and it obviously wasn't Dan, and then you told me you couldn't marry Dan because you loved someone else so I worked out it had to be the scarlet underwear man.'

Tess was so dumfounded she could only stare at him, which she did until Charlotte hiccuped and sent milk spilling down Tess's breast.

Eduardo was on his feet in a flash, taking the baby, handing Tess a handful of tissues, then holding Charlotte gently against his shoulder, rubbing her back as if he'd burped a thousand babies in his time.

Tess looked at them and tears pricked her eyes again, but she was damned if she was going to cry. She was strong, and independent, and she was going to be the best mother in the world to Charlotte, so she couldn't go getting tearful over the sight of the man she loved burping her baby.

'No!' she said.

Eduardo peered down at her, heard a satisfactory burp, handed Charlotte back and waited until Tess settled her on the other breast.

Watching Tess feed her daughter was possibly the best sight in the world, beating even sunsets and sunrises, although feeding little Charlotte himself had rated high on his list of wonders.

Now he shifted his attention from the baby at the breast to her mother.

'No, what?'

Tess sighed as if he was the most terminally stupid man in the world, which he possibly was in matters of love.

'No, the man I love doesn't know I love him, he doesn't have an inkling, and as far as I'm concerned he never will.'

Eduardo absorbed this information. It actually wasn't all that hard to absorb as he was in much the same position, with the woman he loved not knowing of his love.

But he had genuine reasons for not telling her…

'Is he married? Is that why you haven't told him?'

Tess half smiled.

'Is this Twenty Questions?' she asked. 'Because if it is, you've had four.'

'Four? That was only one—or one and a half maybe.'

'It was two, and there were two earlier—have you told him and is he scarlet underwear man? Two more. And for your information, women wear underwear for themselves. It boosts their ego and, believe me, when you're pregnant and looking the size of a council bus, you need all the ego boosting you can get.'

He stared at her, the light tan on her face making her eyes seem greener tonight, the long hair all tousled from sleep, the full mouth that had fed on his with such passion…

With such passion?

Dio! Could it be?

But why would she not say?

Because he'd told her not to expect anything from him…

And what *had* he to offer her?

This answer came more slowly.

Love! He could offer her love.

That's what Rose had pointed out when he'd poured out his heart to her only hours earlier. 'You have love to offer her, Eduardo, and where there's love, all obstacles can be overcome. Do you think she'd be shamed by what has happened in the past? Not that one. She'd stand up and fight anyone who dared to taint your name, she'd tell them you'd been proven innocent, and dare them to say a thing about you. She's a fighter, she's had to be to get to where she is.'

The words were ringing in his head as he reached out and touched Tess on the cheek, pushing a strand of hair back from her face so she couldn't hide behind it.

'Do I have to ask the other sixteen questions to find out who it is?' he asked gently, and she turned and pressed her cheek against his hand.

'I'm going home soon so I guess it doesn't matter,' she whispered, turning her head further so she could press a kiss against his palm. 'And I know you told me all along not to fall in love with you—well, not in so many words but in the way you put yourself down all the time—but how could I help it when you are kind and strong and thoughtful and caring and so damn sexy you'd drive any woman mad?'

She lifted one hand away from the baby and took his, turning so she could face him as she spoke the words.

'I love *you*, Eduardo,' she said quietly, then she tried a smile that damn near broke his heart. 'But quite apart from it not working because you don't love me, it wouldn't work geographically. I know all that. I had the baby partly for her grandparents, so I can't deny them seeing her grow up or deny her having them in her life. Without a father, she'll especially need family. So, you see, it's just one of those things—like Romeo and Juliet—a love that just won't work, although with R. and J., at least they loved each other.'

'Loved each other?' Eduardo echoed weakly, then realised that all Rose had said was true.

'Oh, Tess,' he said, leaning forward to he could kiss her gently on the lips without squashing the baby. 'I love you, too, more than I could ever say.'

He perched on the edge of the bed and held her hand.

'I've used every excuse I could find to tell myself it wouldn't work. I tried staying away from you as much as possible, but how could I not love you, a woman so strong and confident—so beautiful inside and out?'

'Confident? I've been a mess ever since I arrived,' she protested, but she was smiling at him.

'Confident,' he repeated firmly. 'And not afraid to voice your opinion. You were right about it being time for me to return to my other work, and I've already spoken to my old boss about doing just that. The problem is that proven innocence means nothing to some people and I've not wanted to love you, Tess, concerned that, being associated with me, you might be hurt by malicious gossip. That's my biggest worry—that you might suffer.'

She shook her head. 'Just let them try to hurt me or to hurt you,' she said. 'Just let them try!'

He kissed her lips again, but this time she moved away.

'You're going back to your old lab in Brisbane, after all that happened there?' she asked. 'Why do that, when it would be so easy to work in another city—in another country, for that matter?'

How to tell her?

He sat back and smoothed her hair back from her face, then lifted a now sleeping Charlotte from her arms and settled her into the crib by Tess's bed.

'Because it's where you live,' he admitted. 'Loving you

as I do, it was probably a stupid decision, but I thought at least if we were in the same city…'

He stalled and finally admitted, 'I don't know what I thought. I've been in a total mess ever since you arrived, unable to put two consecutive sensible thoughts together.'

'Since I arrived?' Tess queried, unable to believe where her confession had taken them both. Eduardo nodded, slightly shamefaced.

'Pretty much as soon as you arrived,' he admitted. 'I watched you swim that first day, then met you under the palm trees. I was going to send you home but took your hand, and couldn't…'

Tess leaned forward and put her arms around Eduardo.

Could life get any better? She had a daughter, Eduardo loved her, Charlotte would have a father—they'd be a family…

Family! The other one—the other two. Would they all be glad for her?

She drew away from Eduardo, worried now.

'I've lost count of the days—when's Christmas? Can I get home to my family before it? Show them Charlotte? Explain—?'

He bent and kissed her lips to halt her frantic words.

'It's Wednesday, two days to the plane, and, no, my love, you won't be on it. You'll be stuck with me for Christmas— me and Charlotte and Rose and Lila and Hasim and Ramon and Mathilde, who comes back on this week's plane. Then the week after we can both go down to Brisbane.'

Tess wasn't sure if what she felt was disappointment or excitement. Certainly the thought of spending Christmas with Eduardo had an element of delight, and if they kept emailing photos to her parents and the Aldertons…

Although it seemed wrong that they wouldn't share Charlotte's first Christmas…

Eduardo watched the thoughts, happy and sad, chase across her face and guessed what she was thinking. He could tell her now, but that would spoil the surprise and Christmas was only three days away—it wasn't long to wait.

'The best thing you can do,' he told her, 'is to stop fretting over anything and get yourself better, so you're well enough to enjoy a truly Tihoroan Christmas.'

The best Christmas present Tess could possibly have was being told she could leave the little clinic hospital. Rose had brought her clothes, Lila had come to accompany her out the door and, dressed in the blue-green shift she loved, she carried her daughter out the door of the hospital and into the buggy waiting outside.

Eduardo was at the wheel, smiling at her, as well he might, considering the cuddling they'd done very early that morning. But instead of driving her towards her hut, he drove her down the jetty.

'Is it a Christmas ritual that we drive the buggy into the sea?' she teased, feeling so secure in his love she'd trust her life to him. 'Charlotte mightn't like the cold water.'

Eduardo turned to grin at her.

'We're going to the boat. You're coming back to my place. You can't possibly stay in the hut by yourself.'

He stopped the buggy where his boat was moored, with Ramon for once manning the controls. Eduardo took Charlotte while Ramon helped Tess on board, then Eduardo handed her the baby and dropped down. But an even bigger surprise was an ancient sedan chair awaiting them on Eduardo's jetty.

'No way am I getting into that thing,' she told the two men.

'Yes, you are,' Eduardo told her. 'You could burst your stitches, walking up the steps so today you are being carried. My father had it built for my grandmother when her arthritis got too bad for her to manage the steps. She loved Tihoroa.'

'Who wouldn't?' Tess said as she settled herself and Charlotte into the surprisingly comfortable seat and felt herself rising as the two men lifted her.

They set her down where the land levelled out in front of the four low steps leading up to the veranda.

'The last bit you do on your own,' Eduardo told her. 'Go on in. Ramon and I will put away the chair.'

Tess carried Charlotte up the steps, then turned to look back at the vista around her.

'This is part of us now, Charlotte,' she whispered. 'We will come here often.'

Or would they?

Tess tried to think back to the momentous day she and Eduardo had declared their love for each other.

Had he mentioned marriage?

Actually asked her to marry him?

She couldn't remember and surely she would if it had happened.

Doubts assailed her once again, but it was Christmas Day, Charlotte's first Christmas, and nothing was going to spoil it.

She crossed the veranda and entered the huge cool room, her eyes taking a few moments to adjust to the dimmer light.

And when they did, she had to blink and look again. Was she dreaming, or was that her mother beaming at her and holding out her arms, and was that her father standing right beside her, next to Mrs Alderton and Mr Alderton and Dan?

'Mum?' Tess's voice was tentative, sure she must be

dreaming, but the beaming people all came forward, talking at once, saying 'Merry Christmas' and 'Surprise!' and hugging her, taking Charlotte from her arms to pass her around with oohs and aahs of delight.

'Mum?' Tess repeated, checking the baby was secure in Mrs Alderton's arms before tackling the conversation. 'What happened? How did you get here? Why—?'

Her mother hugged her tightly.

'You and Charlotte couldn't come to us so Eduardo suggested we all come to you. Aunt Marj would have been here as well, but Harry's sick. Eduardo flew us all up on the weekly plane and we're staying in the little houses in his garden. On the plane, I sat with Mathilde's mother, who handled the chemo really well and is so positive. But, oh, darling, it's so good to see you and to know you're all right. *And* happy. You are happy, aren't you?'

Tess looked around at her two loving families, their faces lit up with delight over Charlotte. How could she not be happy?

But where was Eduardo? Surely the sedan chair would be put away by now, and if he intended to be her family, wouldn't he be there?

Again she felt a slight quiver of uncertainty, but then he walked in, his eyes searching the room until he found her, smiling at her, silently telling her of his love. But as she went towards him it wasn't to return that message but to hug the child he held by the hand.

Hasim, now well, stood straight and tall on Lila's other side, shyness hidden behind a polite smile.

Tess drew them forward.

'Everyone,' she said, 'I'd like you to meet Lila and Hasim, who are my new good friends.'

But even as she said it, she felt new uncertainty. What would happen to these two? How could she just walk away from Tihoroa not knowing their fate?

Eduardo's arm slid around her and he moved her close to him so he could murmur to her. 'I've got plans,' he said. 'I need to talk to you about them, but I think you'll agree, so stop worrying and enjoy your Christmas.'

Tess looked around her—at her mother holding Lila in her arms, showing her the Christmas tree, while Mrs Alderton was showing Dan Charlotte's tiny fingernails and Mr Alderton was talking with Hasim, who probably didn't understand a word he was saying but was nodding politely anyway.

Across the room, Tess met her father's eyes and he nodded at her, as if to say, Yes, everything's all right.

Ramon summoned them to lunch, served on the back veranda, the smell of roasted pork sizzling in the air, the serving tables laden with salads.

'Happy?' Eduardo asked Tess as he settled her at the head of the table, insisting she was the guest of honour.

'Who wouldn't be?' she answered, then knew he'd sensed her doubts for his fingers tightened on her arms and he dropped a quick kiss on her hair.

'Later,' he whispered.

And she found she was content to wait. She ate lunch with her excited family then Eduardo claimed a now demanding Charlotte, leading Tess into a large but plain bedroom, dominated by a huge four-poster bed with mosquito netting all around it.

To one side a change table had been set up, with nappies and clothes stacked on it, and all the clothes and lotions any baby could ever need.

'Feed Charlotte then have a sleep—doctor's orders.

Your mother and Mrs Alderton want to explore the garden and Ramon will take the men fishing. I'll be here if you need me. I want to show Hasim the lab but Lila wants to stay with you so she'll fetch me, OK?'

He waited until she had settled on the bed, then passed the baby to her, watching as she unfastened her shirt to put Charlotte to her breast.

'I love you, Tess,' he said quietly, then he dropped another kiss on her hair, and one on Charlotte's cheek, and left the room, holding the door open for Lila to come in shyly, before he finally departed.

Lila climbed up on the bed and snuggled close to Tess, as she had so many mornings in the past.

She gently touched a finger to Charlotte's cheek and said, 'Baby,' in a tone of wonder, although she'd been visiting Charlotte as well as Tess every day.

Tess fed the baby, then settled her on the bed, with Lila curled protectively on the other side. Lila sang a lullaby Tess didn't understand but it must have worked for both she and Charlotte slept.

Dinner was fresh fish and lobster grilled on the barbeque, the visitors marvelling that food could taste so good, the men proud of their prowess as providers. Well fed and content, Tess left Charlotte with Eduardo and walked her parents to their guesthouse, assuring her mother yet again that she was happy, although the little doubt still lingered in her mind.

But it was banished early the following morning when Charlotte woke her up for a feed and Eduardo came quietly into the room, having heard the baby cry.

He sat with his arm around Tess as she fed the infant, and talked about doubts and love.

'I wondered,' he admitted, 'in all my dithering about my love for you, if I could love another man's child, but once I'd held her in my hands, I knew that was a stupid thought, for how could I not love her, should I have the chance? I know she's Grant's child, too, and she will know that heritage, but I'll be the best father to her, Tess, I promise you.'

'Father?'

'Of course, father. Do you think I would not marry you? Are you worrying that I haven't asked you formally?'

He ran his fingers through her hair, his smile telling her he was teasing, but love was in his touch, and in his eyes, and Tess felt too embarrassed to admit that, yes, she had been worrying about just that.

'Soon,' he whispered, as she shifted Charlotte to the other breast, and soon the baby fell asleep, a little milky smile on her tiny lips. Eduardo tucked her in a crib he'd produced from somewhere and drew the mosquito netting over it, then took Tess's hand to help her off the bed, wrapped her in a soft terry-towelling robe and led her to the eastern veranda.

A line of light above the sea suggested sunrise must be close. Eduardo settled in a big chair facing the ocean and pulled Tess down on his knee.

'We will share the sunrise, Tess, the first of many,' he said, and she nestled against him, content to feel his love surrounding her.

Then love was forgotten as the line of light grew to an array of colours, deep magenta, glowing orange, purples it would be impossible to paint, stretching along the horizon and reflecting every shade in the calm water below.

And finally a small crescent of molten red, then the sun rose slowly from the sea, seeming to drip its brilliant redness into the water beneath it.

As Tess watched, Eduardo's arms tightened around her, holding her together lest the beauty be too much. His lips nuzzled her neck, then found her ear.

'Will you marry me?' he asked as the sun threw off the night and rode up to claim the sky.

Tess turned towards him.

'You're sure about this?' she said, trying for calm, although her heart was beating a thousand beats a minute and her lungs were choked with happiness.

'Very sure,' he said. 'I love you and I love your daughter, and I know that together, because of our love, we can do anything.'

He kissed her long and hard, then drew back from her, taking her face in the palms of her hands and suddenly looking very serious.

'Speaking of which—the anything—I was wondering…'

What now? Tess thought, her heart stopping altogether.

'About Hasim and Lila,' Eduardo continued. 'Would you mind very much if we added them to our family? I've been talking to Hasim and he was away at university, studying to be a doctor, when his family was killed. I'd like to sponsor them or if necessary adopt them both so they can come with us to Australia and rebuild their lives there.'

Tess couldn't believe what she was hearing—her last worry solved. She put her arms around Eduardo and kissed him hard, unable to find words to express her gratitude.

'Our family's growing,' she whispered.

'And will grow some more,' Eduardo told her, fishing in the pocket of his robe. 'This is my present for Charlotte, but he's in Australia waiting for us, so he doesn't have to go through quarantine when we return.'

He handed Tess a photo of a tiny ball of white fluff, a

little dog, the name Butch printed underneath. And the tears that just kept coming flowed again, tears of happiness that this man who was so caring, so understanding, so generous and thoughtful, actually loved her, Tess Beresford, whose bravest act had been her decision to have Grant's baby.

Now the baby had a father and a dog, a big sister and a brother, and a host of loving relatives.

Family…

It was her turn to take Eduardo's face in her palms, and to tell him of her love and gratitude and how he'd made her life complete, pirating her heart but giving in return the greatest treasure trove of all—abundant love.

MILLS & BOON

MEDICAL

Proudly presents

Brides of Penhally Bay

*A pulse-raising collection of emotional,
tempting romances and heart-warming stories by
bestselling Mills & Boon Medical™ authors.*

January 2008
The Italian's New-Year Marriage Wish
by Sarah Morgan

Enjoy some much-needed winter warmth with
gorgeous Italian doctor Marcus Avanti.

February 2008
The Doctor's Bride By Sunrise
by Josie Metcalfe

Then join Adam and Maggie on a 24-hour rescue mission
where romance begins to blossom as the sun starts to set.

March 2008
The Surgeon's Fatherhood Surprise
by Jennifer Taylor

Single dad Jack Tremayne finds a mother for his
little boy – and a bride for himself.

*Let us whisk you away to an idyllic Cornish town –
a place where hearts are made whole*

COLLECT ALL 12 BOOKS!

100 Reasons to Celebrate

2008 is a very special year as we celebrate Mills and Boon's Centenary.

Each month throughout the year there will be something new and exciting to mark the centenary, so watch for your favourite authors, captivating new stories, special limited edition collections…and more!

www.millsandboon.co.uk

FREE!

4 Books
and a surprise gift!

We would like to take this opportunity to thank you for reading this Mills & Boon® book by offering you the chance to take FOUR more specially selected titles from the Medical™ series absolutely FREE! We're also making this offer to introduce you to the benefits of the Mills & Boon® Reader Service™—

- ★ FREE home delivery
- ★ FREE gifts and competitions
- ★ FREE monthly Newsletter
- ★ Exclusive Reader Service offers
- ★ Books available before they're in the shops

Accepting these FREE books and gift places you under no obligation to buy, you may cancel at any time, even after receiving your free shipment. Simply complete your details below and return the entire page to the address below. You don't even need a stamp!

YES! Please send me 4 free Medical books and a surprise gift. I understand that unless you hear from me, I will receive 6 superb new titles every month for just £2.89 each, postage and packing free. I am under no obligation to purchase any books and may cancel my subscription at any time. The free books and gift will be mine to keep in any case.

M7ZEF

Ms/Mrs/Miss/Mr ....Initials ....

BLOCK CAPITALS PLEASE

Surname ....

Address ....

....Postcode ....

Send this whole page to:
UK: FREEPOST CN81, Croydon, CR9 3WZ